FLIP-IT-OVER
GUIDES TO TEEN EMOTIONS

A Guys' Guide to

Anger

Hal Marcovitz

Enslow Publishers, Inc.
40 Industrial Road
Box 398
Berkeley Heights, NJ 07922
USA

http://www.enslow.com

Library of Congress Cataloging-in-Publication Data

Marcovitz, Hal.
   A guys' guide to anger ; A girls' guide to anger / Hal Marcovitz and Gail Snyder.
      p. cm. — (Flip-it-over guides to teen emotions)
   Includes bibliographical references and index.
   ISBN-13: 978-0-7660-2853-1
   ISBN-10: 0-7660-2853-4
   1. Anger—Juvenile literature. 2. Boys—Life skills guides—Juvenile literature. 3. Girls—Life skills guides—Juvenile literature. I. Snyder, Gail. II. Title. III. Title: Guys' guide to anger ; A girls' guide to anger. IV. Title: Girls' guide to anger.
   BF575.A5M33 2008
   155.42'4247—dc22

                                2007026459

Printed in the United States of America.
112009 Lake Book Manufacturing, Inc., Melrose Park, IL

10 9 8 7 6 5 4 3 2

Produced by OTTN Publishing, Stockton, N.J.

To Our Readers: We have done our best to make sure all Internet Addresses in this book were active and appropriate when we went to press. However, the author and the publisher have no control over and assume no liability for the material available on those Internet sites or on other Web sites they may link to. Any comments or suggestions can be sent by e-mail to comments@enslow.com or to the address on the title page.

Photo Credits: © Digital Vision, 28; © iStockphoto.com/Leslie Banks, 19; © iStockphoto.com/Jani Bryson, 38; © iStockphoto.com/Clayton Hansen, 45; © iStockphoto.com/Eileen Hart, 48; © iStockphoto.com/Ed Hidden, 18; © iStockphoto.com/Nicholas Monu, 22; © iStockphoto.com/Aldo Murillo, 40; © iStockphoto.com/Bobbie Osborne, 6; © iStockphoto.com/Roberta Osborne, 1; © iStockphoto.com/TriggerPhoto, 52; © iStockphoto.com/Lisa F. Young, 25, 29, 34; © 2008 Jupiterimages Corporation, 51; Library of Congress, 57 (both); Used under license from Shutterstock, Inc., 3, 4, 8, 12 (both), 15, 17, 21, 24, 26, 32, 37, 43, 46, 50, 55.

Cover Photo: © iStockphoto.com/Roberta Osborne.

CONTENTS

CHAPTER ONE

What Is Anger?

> This morning Derek's older brother Kyle said he'd pick Derek up after basketball practice, around 4:30 P.M. Practice ended on time and soon afterward Derek was outside the school, wishing his brother hadn't insisted that he wait outdoors. It was freezing and he didn't have his jacket.
>
> Twenty minutes later Kyle's car finally pulled up to the curb. Shivering in the cold, Derek swung the car door open, shouting angrily, "What took you so long? It's freezing out here. Where were you?" Derek realized he was breathing fast and his clenched hands were shaking.

Everybody gets angry at one time or another. And Derek was no exception. He was so angry at his brother for keeping him waiting that he started yelling as soon as he got in the car.

Anger is a common human emotion—it's a normal response when you feel something has hurt or threatened you. Anger makes you feel like you have to do something—and fast. When you feel angry you may feel like you have to break something, or yell about the situation, or shove the person bugging you. But these ways of showing anger often create more problems. You've made other people angry with you. And afterwards, you are likely to feel pretty rotten about your harmful words or actions.

You and Your Emotions

A part of everyone's personality, emotions are a powerful driving force in life. They are hard to define and understand. But what is known is that emotions—which include anger, fear, love, joy, jealousy, and hate—are a normal part of the human system. They are responses to situations and events that trigger bodily changes, motivating you to take some kind of action.

Some studies show that the brain relies more on emotions than on intellect in learning and in making decisions. Being able to identify and understand the emotions in yourself and in others can help you in your relationships with family, friends, and others throughout your life.

When you are angry, your body becomes agitated and energized. Your blood pressure rises. Your heart beats faster. Your body temperature rises, so you start sweating. Your breathing becomes heavier and more rapid. Your muscles become tense.

What Happens When You Get Mad?

When you are angry, your body produces larger amounts of certain hormones—special chemical substances that can influence behavior and mood. The hormone adrenaline increases the rate of blood flowing through your body, while another hormone, cortisol, gives a quick burst of energy.

Anger is part of your body's protective response to threat or danger.

All these symptoms of anger are part of your body's protective response to threat or danger. The body feels strong and ready for action, or better able to physically defend itself. "Anger prepares us for action," explains psychology researcher Carroll E. Izard. "It bolsters physical strength and courage to match the impulse to act. We may never feel stronger or more invigorated than when we are really angry."[1]

This feeling of being ready to stand and fight—or to run away—dates back to prehistoric times. Known as the "fight-or-flight" instinct, it allowed primitive people to confront and survive dangers from wild animals and other threats. Although you don't typically need to defend yourself from wild animals today, your body still responds the same way

When faced with a situation that makes you angry, you are responsible for the actions you choose to take in response and the results of those actions.

whenever you feel threatened or uncomfortable.

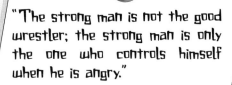

"The strong man is not the good wrestler; the strong man is only the one who controls himself when he is angry."

—The Prophet Muhammad

You may feel angry when you are unsure of how to react in a confusing situation. Your anger may be prompted by a threat from another person or if you feel someone did something to hurt you. You may feel angry because you did poorly on a test or in a game. Anger is a normal response to when you believe a friend has let you down. It can also be a reaction to injustice, fear, or feeling out of control.

An angry response is more likely to happen whenever you're feeling overwhelmed by other emotions such as disappointment, grief, or fear. In the same way, stress—a feeling of emotional strain caused by demanding circumstances—can also lead to anger. For example, suppose you may have a fast-approaching homework assignment, and you're feeling stressed over having to meet the deadline. You may be angry at yourself for not getting the work done earlier. Or you may direct your anger at your friends who knew you had the assignment but talked you into going to the movies instead of working on it. Or you may feel angry with the teacher for assigning the project in the first place.

A Rush of Adrenaline Causes:

1. Shortness of breath
2. Flushed skin
3. Rigid, tensed muscles
4. Tightened jaw, shoulders, hands
5. Fragmented thoughts
6. Agitation
7. Trembling

Anger can be a good thing if it helps give you the confidence to assert yourself in a stressful situation or if someone threatens you or puts you down. However, the way that you express yourself when angry is important. Most people learn to deal with their anger and calm down within a few seconds or minutes. But sometimes people can't control their anger.

Anger becomes a problem when it is released in ways that cause harm to others, whether through physical violence, temper tantrums, or verbal abuse. That's aggression, and it's not a good thing—for you or the person on the receiving end. Washington, D.C. psychologist Carole Stovall points out that anger does not need to lead to aggression: "It's important for people to keep in mind that while anger is a feeling that everybody has, aggression is a choice. Aggression is a behavior that we learn to engage in, and we can learn not to engage in it."[2] In other words, you can learn how to express anger in ways that are not harmful to others.

Feeling stressed out over schoolwork and a busy schedule can make you feel like snapping out in anger.

Science Says...

Researchers at the University of Massachusetts say most people get angry at least several times a week. Some said they had angry feelings several times a day. About 60 percent of them are able to calm themselves down, while 39 percent will approach the people responsible for making them angry in an attempt to resolve the situation. [3]

When people are angry, they may try talking to another person who is not involved with the conflict. But studies show that almost half say they raise their voice when angry, while 10 percent become physically aggressive. That is, they hit, strike, or shove the person they're angry with. [4]

If you don't learn to control your anger, you risk letting your anger control you. But you can learn how to control your anger if you want to. What's important is that you understand how your anger affects you.

You're More Likely to Get Angry...

- If you're in poor health.

- If you haven't had enough sleep.

- If you're feeling overwhelmed by stress, disappointment, grief, or fear.

CHAPTER TWO

Are You Quick to Anger?

> The school hallway was mobbed. While trying to avoid a class door that opened suddenly, Carlos stumbled and accidentally bumped into Dylan. Dylan exploded. "You moron!" he exclaimed. He grabbed Carlos's arm and with a hard stare warned, "Don't ever do that again, do you understand?"
>
> Wow, Carlos thought to himself as he continued walking down the hall. What's his problem?

Some people are quick to anger. That is, they are always ready to take offense, often about incidents that wouldn't make another person think twice. How a person experiences and expresses anger—as well as other emotions—is a part of temperament and personality. Someone with a laid-back personality is less likely to have an anger meltdown than someone with an aggressive personality.

Do you take offense easily? Are you quick to anger? Check out the quiz on page 11. As you read each statement, give an honest response. Then, add up your score.

A score of 12 or higher may indicate that you have some aggressive tendencies. That is, you are easily irritated and often express your anger in ways that don't take other people's feelings into account. In fact, people you know may consider you difficult

"Anger is that powerful internal force that blows out the light of reason."

—Ralph Waldo Emerson

Do You Get Angry Easily?

Read each sentence and indicate how strongly you agree with the statement. Give yourself 3 points (often); 2 points (sometimes); 1 point (seldom); and 0 points (never).

1. It annoys me when I have to wait in line or wait for other people.

2. People say I lose my temper a lot.

3. It irritates me when people don't do what I think they should do or when things don't go my way.

4. I hold a grudge against people who have hurt me.

5. I have gotten into trouble at school because of my temper.

6. Some people are afraid of me because of my temper.

7. I have said or done some hurtful things to others when angry.

8. My way is usually the best way of doing things.

If your score is less than 12, you have a handle on your anger. A score of 12 or more indicates that it's time to reevaluate how you get along with other people.

An aggressive response often leads to hard feelings among all involved.

to get along with. They might describe you as having a problem with anger.

The aggressive personality. People with aggressive personalities tend to be critical and controlling of others. When they don't get their own way, they think it's okay to explode in anger, lashing out with insults, sarcastic comments, threats, and even physical violence at the person they blame for their problems. When they hurt someone in anger—whether emotionally or physically— they don't take responsibility for their actions, but instead place all blame on that person. Afterwards, they may forget about their meltdown and expect the target of their rage to do the same.

Passive and passive-aggressive. People who don't show their anger may have a passive personality. By being passive, they are accepting without question or resistance whatever others say or do. Passive people tend to have trouble

A passive approach is to ignore the problem—and keep your anger inside.

dealing with conflict, so they usually keep silent, even when they don't agree with the decisions that are being made for them. Essentially, people who have passive behavior are putting the rights of others before their own rights. This doesn't mean they don't get angry. They either keep their emotions bottled up inside or they become passive-aggressive.

The Consequences of Being Aggressive

When people lose complete control of their behavior, their rage can have serious consequences. In addition to losing the respect of their friends, they might also face other penalties. For example, during a nationally televised basketball game against the Detroit Pistons in November 2004, Indiana Pacer Ron Artest charged furiously into the stands. Thinking one of the spectators had thrown a cup at him, Artest violently attacked the man. By the time the fight ended, at least nine people had been injured.

Artest's aggressive actions caused him to be suspended from the league. As a result, he missed eighty-six regular season and playoff games—which cost him almost $5 million in salary. He also had to serve a year of probation, perform fifty hours community service, attend anger management counseling, and pay a $250 fine.

Traded to the LA Kings in January 2006, Artest welcomed having the chance to start anew: "I'm going to play hard," he said. "That's all I can do. Things that were distractions to my team in the past—I've learned from my mistakes, and I look forward to those things not happening."[1]

Aggressive, Passive, or Assertive?

Choose the answer that best describes how you would behave in each of the following situations:

1. Your friend keeps interrupting with advice and comments when you're showing your new video game to the other guys.

    A. Give him a shove and tell him to cut it out.

    B. Let him talk. After all, he already owns the game and knows how to play it.

    C. Tell him that you want to show the features you know first. Then he can have a turn.

2. Your coach yelled at you in front of the other players for not passing the ball more often.

    A. Yell back at the coach and tell him he doesn't know what he's talking about.

    B. Say nothing but go home and complain to your parents that night.

    C. After practice, ask the coach if you can talk about what happened.

3. Your little sister took your CD without asking, broke the case, and didn't apologize.

    A. Take one of her CDs, break the case, and leave it on her bed.

    B. Say nothing.

    C. Let her know you're bothered and ask for an apology.

4. You made plans to meet Marco at the movies and he just called at the last minute to cancel. The same thing happened last weekend, and the weekend before that.

   A. Tell him you're tired of his excuses and to forget about ever going to a movie together again.

   B. Say that's okay. Maybe you can go next weekend instead.

   C. Ask him why he keeps canceling on you. Is he having problems at home?

5. Your friend borrowed money from you more than a month ago and still hasn't paid you back.

   A. Tell him to pay up by the end of the day . . . or else.

   B. Say nothing at all and accept that you won't be getting anything back.

   C. Explain to your friend that you need the money now. Ask how and when he plans to pay you back.

If most of your answers were A's, you are being aggressive; B's reflect a passive or passive-aggressive behavior; while C's reflect assertive responses, which are more likely to have good results!

When people behave in a passive-aggressive way, they don't directly confront the person who made them angry. Instead they think of ways to get even. A passive-aggressive person may complain to others and spread lies and rumors about the offending person. So it is possible that a person who behaves in a passive way could also score high on the anger quiz.

In any case, a high score on the quiz indicates a need for you to learn better ways of dealing with your anger. Aggressive, passive, and passive-aggressive behaviors are not good ways to handle anger.

Assertive. If you had a low score on the quiz, you most likely have a healthier way of dealing with your anger—the assertive approach. When you are assertive, you express yourself honestly and in a manner that respects the rights of others. Instead of flying off the handle, you think over the issue and come up with the best response. You aren't afraid to speak out if you feel you have been wronged.

Just because you behaved a certain way in the past doesn't mean you are locked into that personality for the rest of your life. However, if you see that your behavior is a problem for you and in your relationships with others, you may want to change. And you'll find that using assertive behavior in managing your anger can give you the best results.

Anger

Learned behavior. Personality isn't the only thing influencing how people express anger. Young children learn how to behave in certain situations based on watching how their parents and other family behave. If they grow up seeing aggressive behavior, they may believe that aggression is normal, acceptable behavior.

Similarly, American society gives messages to guys that they're supposed to be aggressive. As a result, many guys believe that walking away from an argument or a fight is a sign of weakness. Violence is never the answer. There are ways to express your anger without hurting others. Your anger shouldn't stop you from getting along with friends, family, and others. When you learn how to manage your anger, they'll feel better about you, and you'll feel better about yourself.

If kids grow up in households where anger is expressed by yelling and screaming, they are likely to imitate that behavior.

CHAPTER THREE

When You're Mad at Yourself

> Pete had studied very hard for his math quiz and thought he'd done well. But when he got the test back, he'd gotten just about every answer wrong. Pete was so angry that he tore up the paper. From then on, he stopped paying attention in class and didn't do any more homework.
>
> When Pete's parents saw the failing grade on his report card, they wanted to know what was going on. "It doesn't do me any good to study," Pete told them, "I'm too stupid."

Pete let his anger with himself drag him down. Instead of dealing with his problems, he withdrew and ignored them. He decided he wasn't any good at anything and simply gave up trying.

Dealing with anger and disappointment by withdrawing from the world is a typical reaction for somebody who has little self-respect, or self-esteem. People with low self-esteem don't think they can overcome challenges. Instead, they give up and consider themselves failures.

Other emotions were affecting Pete's behavior. He was feeling shame at failing the test he had studied hard for. And he felt guilty for not living up to his parents' expectations.

"Holding on to anger is like grasping a hot coal with the intent of throwing it at someone else; you are the one who gets burned."

—Buddha

However, when Pete's parents learned about his problems with math, they were a lot more understanding than Pete had believed they would be. They met with Pete's teacher and arranged for their son to get some extra help in math. The extra tutoring paid off in several ways. Not only was Pete able to better understand what was going on in math class but he also found himself a lot less angry.

Pete realized that he should have talked to his parents much earlier—in fact as soon as he ran into trouble. Talking his problems over with them would have been a positive step in defusing his anger.

Don't be afraid to talk to your parents. That's what they are there for. You'll feel a lot better once you get things off your chest.

CHAPTER FOUR

When You're Angry with Friends

> Zach was joking with his friend Damian in the cafeteria before school started. "So I hear you like Megan and you're going to ask her out."
>
> Damian rolled his eyes. Zach had been on his case about Megan all week. "What are you saying? You know that's not true," he replied.
>
> Zachary continued, "Yeah, you know you do, too. Everybody knows—"
>
> Damian leaned forward and glared at Zach. "I said, cut it out. I mean it!" he yelled.

Even the best of friends can get angry with each other. Sometimes when friends joke, or tease each other, one of them may cross the line and cause hard feelings. A teammate may get angry with a team member for not playing his best in a game. A friend may forget to repay a loan. Someone may feel slighted because the group spent time together playing video games—and didn't think to call him up to invite him. With many guys, the first reaction to anger is to respond physically—with a push, a shove, or even a punch. But there are better ways to express anger.

Reevaluate the situation. Even if you think you have a good reason for becoming aggressive, step back and think about it. Is it really worthwhile losing your temper? This can be especially true if you are in school and will have to pay the consequences—such as detention or suspension—

Before you get angry with a friend, be sure to get the full story. Don't risk losing a friendship because of a misunderstanding.

for fighting while on school grounds. Before you blow up, consider what an aggressive response would achieve:

- If you think your friend has cheated you, get the facts straight: Has the person really cheated you, or have you just misjudged the situation?

- If someone did something that hurt you, think about what happened. Perhaps whatever that person did to you wasn't intentional—it was just a mistake on his or her part.

- If you get angry and lash out at this person, will you regret it later?

- Will you really solve anything by expressing your anger aggressively? After you chew the person out, you may find yourself still unhappy or grumpy.

When You're Angry with Friends

- If you raise your voice or even hit someone, will you get your way or will nothing change? Chances are, venting your rage won't solve anything.

- Is flying off the handle your way of demanding your rights?

- By getting mad, are you out to prove something? Are you trying to show everyone that you can't be pushed around?

- By raising your voice, talking tough, and using bad words, are you trying to make people respect you? In fact, after watching you throw a tantrum, they will probably have less respect for you.[1]

Get another perspective. If you are feeling really angry, you might benefit from talking to someone who isn't

Venting Doesn't Get Anger Out of Your System

Research has shown that screaming, yelling, and hitting pillows isn't the best way to make feelings of anger disappear.[2] People who hit punching bags and rage loudly against others may believe that venting their anger makes them less angry. However, studies show that their loud outbursts are actually making them feel more justified with their anger and they become even more hostile and aggressive. Meantime, the person who is being yelled at becomes defensive and hostile as well.[3]

involved with the issue at all. Try calling someone you trust to talk about what is troubling you. After you talk over the issue with a third party, you may find yourself less angry.

However, if you are concerned about burdening your friend with your problems, you may find the best approach would be to have a conversation with the person with whom you're angry. That means talking—calmly and quietly—with that person in order help him or her understand your issue.

Have a conversation that includes "I-messages." These are solution-oriented statements that don't place blame, but simply allow you to tell someone how you feel. I-messages focus on how the problem affects you and what you would like to see happen to fix things. An I-message has four basic parts:

- "I *feel*…" (States the emotions you are feeling.)

- "…*when*…" (Gives details about what the other person did or said that caused the hard feelings.)

- "…*because*…" (Explains why you feel that way. This can be the hardest part of the I-message.)

- "I *want*…" (Describes what you think will resolve the conflict or ease the bad feelings.)

What Triggers Anger?

- Not being listened to or respected
- Feeling left out
- Being cheated or lied to
- Feeling rejected or controlled by others
- Feeling embarrassed
- Being blamed for something you didn't do
- Being hurt or threatened

Instead of yelling at Zach because of his teasing, for example, Damian could have used an I-message to let him know how he felt. An example would be: "I feel really angry when you tease me about girls because I think that's private stuff. I want you to stop." What's most important is that Damian talk to his friend to let him know there is a problem.

When discussing conflicts with people, you don't have to convince them you are right and they are wrong. It is enough just to let them know that you are troubled. You need to keep talking to your friends, even when you're angry. By keeping the lines of communication open, you will eventually find a solution to your problem.

Resolving conflicts with siblings. Just as friends can get angry with one another, so can siblings. The reasons can vary. An older brother may think his parents aren't being fair about house rules regarding curfew or family chores. A younger brother may be jealous that his big brother is a superstar athlete. Feelings of competition between brothers and sisters—or sibling rivalry—can often lead to hard feelings in families. But one of the biggest issues can be when one sibling feels that the other doesn't show respect.

It is perfectly normal to feel angry with brothers and sisters from

Take a few minutes to compose yourself and your thoughts before speaking in the heat of anger.

Think About It

Once you are able to understand what is making you angry, you will have the ability to better control your actions when you get mad. Ask yourself:

What set me off?
How did I feel?
What were my thoughts?
What did I want to do?

time to time. However, when siblings treat each other badly—by insulting, cursing at, pushing, and hitting—the bad feelings will continue. Instead, it is important to try to mend your relationship by showing respect when talking to each other.

Have a conversation in which you use I-messages, so that you are not blaming your brother or sister for something that will make him or her feel defensive. Using I-messages will let your sibling know you have a problem that you're trying to fix.

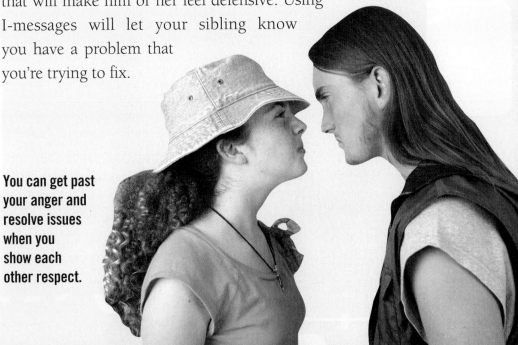

You can get past your anger and resolve issues when you show each other respect.

CHAPTER FIVE

When Adults Make You Mad

At age thirteen, Tad thought he was old enough to attend a rock concert with his friends, but his mother disagreed. Concerned that drugs and alcohol would be abused at the concert, Tad's mother made him stay home. Tad was furious. "She treats me like a little kid," he told his friends. After arguing with his mother, Tad ran to his room, slammed the door, and locked it.

A major cause of feeling angry with parents is your changing relationship. It is natural at this point in your life to want more independence. However, parents can sometimes have a hard time accepting that need for independence. They have been in charge of you for many years. And they are concerned about you and your safety.

However, you may be feeling more strongly and more often about doing what you want to do—not what adults are telling you to do. When your wishes conflict with those of your parents and other adults, it is not unusual for both of you to feel angry with one another.

There can be other reasons besides conflicts for feeling angry with parents. For example, they may have high

You can feel angry when it seems like the adults in your life are always telling you what to do.

expectations of you that you don't feel capable of achieving—in school, sports, music, or other areas. They may have made promises that they have been unable to keep. Or they may be making demands on your time—such as requiring that you babysit your little sister every afternoon after school, which means you can't participate in any after-school activities.

"Keep cool; anger is not an argument."

—Daniel Webster

What is important is the way that you express your desire for more freedom or question your parents' authority over your life. If you yell at them, you probably won't have much success. Instead, when you have a conflict with your parents—or any adult for that matter—try to address it in a healthy way.

First of all, calm down. If you need to, leave the room. Don't come back until you're ready to talk calmly. Then, being careful to stay calm and respectful, explain your point of view. In other words, talk with your parents the same way you

Failing to Meet Parents' Expectations

Sometimes parents seem like they expect their child to be the best athlete, top scholar, or accomplished musician. If you feel your folks are being unrealistic in their expectations and standards for you, don't get angry. Talk to them. Let them know that you're trying your best, but that they have to accept you as you are.

If You Have a Conflict with Your Teacher

Disagreements with teachers do happen.

But what if you feel the teacher is picking on you? If you think your teacher has been unfair to you, the best thing to do is try to talk to him or her. Stay calm as you explain your case. Afterward, if you still believe your issue is not resolved, talk to your parents. If they agree with you, they will probably want to talk to the teacher themselves.

would like them to talk to you. You stand a better chance of changing their minds if they can see that you can deal with disagreements in a calm, sensible way.

The same holds true for disagreements you may have with the coach who benches you or with the teacher who isn't satisfied with your work and makes you stay after school. These adults have their reasons for making you do what you don't want to do. Rather than getting angry with them and storming off, you will get better results by asking to talk with them. See some more suggestions on page 31 on talking with adults.

Family changes. Sometimes teens can get mad at parents when their actions cause major family upheavals. Among the most serious family changes are separations and divorce. The breakup of a family can be painful, especially if there are hard feelings between the mother and father—some teens feel angry with their parents for being unable to work out their differences. And sometimes kids feel anger towards the parent who initiated the breakup.

New issues can arise when a divorced parent remarries and forms a new household. With the addition of a new set of family members, conflict can also occur. For example, eleven-year-old John was constantly fighting with his stepmother. She tried very hard to get along with her stepson, but he found fault with everything she did. He didn't like the meals she prepared for him, and he didn't like being told to clean up his room. When she told him to be home at a certain time, he ignored her and stayed out late.

John really wasn't angry with his stepmother. He was angry with his mother for divorcing his father and leaving the family. Since his mother no longer lived with him or showed any interest in seeing him again, John could not express his anger toward her. It was only after he was able to explain these feelings to his father and stepmother that things got better. They were understanding, and made an effort as well to help John deal with his anger.

How you behave during a conflict will affect its outcome.

Dealing with an Angry Parent

- Stay calm and quiet. If your parent or another adult has lost his or her temper with you, recognize that the person isn't thinking clearly. Don't try to explain yourself just yet. Anything you say may anger the adult even more.

- After the angry adult seems to have calmed down, explain how you felt about being on the receiving end of his or her anger. In a respectful, nonjudgmental voice, talk about how undeserved rage is affecting you.

- Ask your parent if he or she can set aside some time for an activity—a walk or a drive—during which you can talk. It might be worthwhile to bring up the idea of family therapy or counseling.

- If parents (or other adults) are physically abusive toward you or someone you know, you need to get help. Talk to a trusted adult such as a school guidance counselor or call the domestic violence hotline listed on page 61.

Still, divorce is just one of the many family life changes that cause tensions in households. Other changes in a person's home life—such as a move to a new city or the death or long illness of a family member—can also spark feelings of anger. If your mother or father takes a job in a different city, and forces the family to move, you may get angry with your parents for making you leave your friends behind.

Whatever the cause of your anger, remember that the best way to deal with it is to try to take charge of it. Try to solve any problems resulting from the change so you feel better about the future. Talking about conflict with the adults in your life can be a big help. If you express your anger by refusing to talk to others and by locking yourself away in your room, you won't change anything.

Tips on Talking to Parents, Coaches, and Other Adults

Bring up your issue when the adult has the time to listen. Ask, "Is this a good time for you? I have something important to discuss."

Be aware of your body language. Don't roll your eyes, cross your arms, or clench your fists.

Use respectful language. Avoid sarcasm, put-downs, and insults.

Be honest. Tell the truth about how you feel or what has happened.

Show respect and listen to the other side of the story. The adult will be more likely to show you the same respect.

CHAPTER SIX

I'm Not Taking It Anymore!

Ryan is a lot bigger than Alex, even though they are the same age. Ryan is also very competitive, and he is angry with Alex for getting the top grades in science. Last month, he started insulting the smaller boy, calling him a "nerd" whenever he passed in him the hall. Yesterday, at the end of science lab, Ryan stole Alex's backpack and tossed it in the trash when no one was looking.

School bullies make life miserable for the kids they target. They want to hurt their victims, and typically do so with verbal and physical aggression. This includes using taunts, insults, and name-calling that typically focuses on appearance—weight, height, or clothing, for example. Bullying may also involve spreading rumors or gossiping at school and over the Internet. It can include intimidating or frightening the victim into doing what the bully wants—such as turning over money or telling answers to homework or tests. And it may involve pushing, shoving, and hitting.

Typically, bullies act the way they do in order to feel power—to feel that they are

Being bullied would make anyone angry.

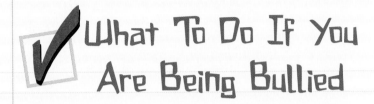

What To Do If You Are Being Bullied

1. Unless you believe you may be physically harmed, confront your tormentor. Look the bully in the eye and tell him, firmly and clearly, to stop.

2. Then get away from the situation as quickly as possible.

3. Tell an adult what has happened immediately. If you are afraid to tell a teacher on your own, ask a friend to go with you.

4. Keep on speaking up until you get someone to listen. Explain what happened, who was involved, where it occurred, and what you have done.

5. Remember, bullying is not your fault—don't blame yourself for what has happened.[1]

better than the kids they are picking on. Bullies may attack because they are angry that they are not as good at something as their victim. Or they may feel justified in terrorizing someone else because they feel angry over some real or imagined

It is normal for the targets of bullying to feel angry. But be aware that the bully typically wants to see you flip out or explode in anger. This means the bully is in control of your behavior, not you.

insult. Other times, they bully because they are prejudiced— that is, they have decided they don't like a person because of his or her specific race, religion, or ethnicity. They express their anger toward a racial, religious, or ethnic group by beating up, harassing, or teasing a person who is a member.

Sometimes, a bully is frustrated with problems at home or at school and takes out his anger on a younger, weaker person. Psychologists call this "displaced anger"—when anger is

Don't ignore a bully in hopes that he'll stop. Let others know what's going on.

directed at someone who has had nothing to do with the situation. Displaced anger can also turn victims of bullies into bullies themselves, if they take out their frustrations on someone smaller and weaker than them.

In addition to being angry at the person who is tormenting him, the victim of a bully can feel a range of other unsettling emotions that may last over weeks, months, and even years. One of the strongest is fear, accompanied by constant worry and anxiety, that the bully will embarrass him with taunts and jeers or even carry out threats of physical violence. Other unbearable feelings can include shame and guilt—and a sense of helplessness—over the victim's lack ability to change the situation.

Feelings of anger resulting from being bullied can lead to serious problems. In some cases, anger directed at a bully can lead the victim to plot ways to get revenge. However, this course of action won't solve any issues, and often results in additional pain and troubles. Just as serious can be the problems that result when anger is directed within—when the victim of bullying is furious with himself for not being "strong enough" or "brave enough" to fight back. The following chapter describes how bottled-up anger and low self-esteem can be dangerous.

CHAPTER SEVEN

Bottled-Up Anger

Michael has been struggling with his classes lately, and his father is angry with him for bringing home poor grades. Michael's mother hasn't really noticed his grades because she's been too busy looking after his younger sisters, who have been sick.

School has been difficult in other ways, too. Michael isn't very athletic and really hates going to gym class. The teacher has insisted that he show improvement or he'll get a failing grade. Many of the other guys in the class think this is pretty funny, and have started picking on him.

Each day, when Michael returns home from school, he goes upstairs to his room and remains there for hours. He tells his parents he's studying, but instead he spends his time sitting by himself, thinking about how he is really a loser.

Michael is angry with a lot of people. He is mad at his father for not understanding his academic struggles. He is angry at his mother for being too busy for him. He is mad at his gym teacher for not understanding how much he hates gym and at the boys who are teasing him. And he hates himself for not being able to do anything about his life.

Because Michael believes that he can't change his situation, he hasn't tried to do anything about it. Instead he has isolated himself from others and

"An angry man is always full of poison."

—Confucius

Keeping anger inside can lead to depression.

suppressed his emotions, effectively numbing himself from feeling anything. He has few friends at school or in his neighborhood, but he says that he prefers to be alone.

Denying anger and suppressing emotions can be dangerous because this behavior can lead to more serious problems. A common result of keeping anger inside is depression—extreme feelings of sadness and hopelessness.

The long-term suppression of anger, particularly when a

Anger Directed Inward Can Cause:

- Physical self-harm
- Feelings of depression and guilt
- Emotional numbness
- Drug, alcohol, food, or other forms of addiction

Some Symptoms of Depression

- Loss of interest in favorite activities
- Ongoing feelings of sadness and hopelessness
- Irritability and anger
- Fatigue and reduced energy
- Physical illnesses (stomachaches and headaches that don't respond to treatment)
- Reduced ability to function in social situations (with friends, at school, and in other places)
  - Frequent absences from school or poor performance in classes
  - Changes in eating or sleeping habits
  - Trouble concentrating or following a conversation

person has low self-esteem, can lead to a serious illness called clinical depression. This mental disorder is diagnosed when feelings of sadness, hopelessness, and fatigue last for more than two weeks. Individuals suffering from clinical depression tend to withdraw from participating in activities with friends. They may stop doing schoolwork or even going to school. Severely depressed teens don't share their feelings with others, because they believe that no one really cares about them. Like Michael, they spend much of their time alone.

Because clinical depression distorts a person's thinking, it can lead to self-destructive actions. Severely depressed people may be irritable and edgy—often ready to take their anger out on family members or anyone who tries to help. Their sense of low self-worth can lead them to engage in dangerous behaviors such as heavy drug and alcohol use. They are also more likely to become addicted to harmful substances or to suffer from eating disorders.

Warning Signs of Suicide

- Talk about suicide or death

- Obsession with death and the afterlife

- Withdrawal from friends or family

- Preference for being alone

- Changes in eating and sleeping habits

- Talk about feeling hopeless, worthless, or guilty

- Reckless or self-destructive behavior (such as abuse of alcohol or drugs)

- Loss of interest in hobbies, sports or other activities

- Giving away important possessions

- Talk about "going away"

Clinical depression has also been known to cause teens to physically harm themselves and even commit suicide. When drug or alcohol use is involved, this risk of self-harm is increased. According to the U.S. Centers for Disease Control and Prevention (CDC), the third leading cause of death among fifteen- to twenty-five-year-olds in 2004 was teen suicide, and 86 percent of all teenage suicides were guys.[1]

If you think your friend is depressed, talk to him and let him know there are ways to get help.

Anger

A Call for Help

Suicide crisis lines are toll-free lines that are staffed twenty-four hours a day, seven days a week by trained professionals. They provide information and support to people who are in need of help or who are trying to figure what to do to help a friend. If you believe a friend is suicidal, call the hotline listed on page 61.

If you are feeling depressed, don't ignore your feelings. Talk about them with someone you trust—a good friend, your parents, a school counselor, or a religious leader. Don't be afraid to ask for help.

Similarly, if you're worried that a friend is showing symptoms of depression, let him or her know that you're concerned. If you believe that your friend is showing warning signs of suicide, you need to take action. Tell a trusted adult about your suspicions or call an emergency telephone hotline number.

Depression is a treatable illness, but recovery takes a long time. Successfully overcoming severe depression requires the care of a mental health professional such as a psychiatrist—a medical doctor specially trained to diagnose and treat mental illnesses. He or she will typically prescribe antidepressant medication, and individual and family therapy. The compassion and support of family and friends can also help a person suffering from depression get better.

CHAPTER EIGHT

Taking Charge of Your Anger

When Philip didn't turn in his homework in science class, his teacher, Mrs. Trautman, rolled her eyes and sighed, "Don't tell me you forgot your homework again." Without thinking, Philip shouted back at her, "Oh, just leave me alone! I had better things to do last night than homework!" His loud outburst got him sent to the principal's office.

From there, things got worse. Philip's mother, a busy store manager, was called away from work to pick up her son at school. That night, Philip argued with his parents. They told him that he could not play video games or watch TV until he finished all of his homework. Philip was angry. "You have no right to tell me what to do! It's not fair!" he yelled at his parents as he stormed out of the room. His parents grounded him for the week.

By expressing his anger with yelling and name-calling, Philip made a bad situation worse. If he had been able to manage his anger, it is likely that the outcome could have been different: he wouldn't have ended up in the principal's offices or been stuck at home over the weekend. These punishments didn't really help Philip change his behavior, though. What he needed was a lesson on anger management.

"Speak when you are angry and you will make the best speech you will ever regret."

—Ambrose Bierce

Anger cues. People who teach anger management skills suggest that you work to change how you

A big part of managing anger is understanding what caused it in the first place. If you are fearful, hurt, disappointed, guilty, or sad, these feelings may prompt you to feel anger.

respond when someone says or does something that angers you. Learn to recognize the signs that you are beginning to feel anger—your anger cues. They help you know that you need to pause and think about why you are becoming angry.

During this time think about whether any other emotions, such as fear or anxiety, may be fueling your anger. Philip may have lashed out at his teacher because he was feeling guilty at messing up once again. If he had simply

Flying off the handle and yelling will never make a situation better.

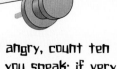

> "When angry, count ten before you speak; if very angry, a hundred."
>
> —Thomas Jefferson

promised the teacher that he would do a better job on keeping up with his homework, he could have avoided more problems.

Think ahead. Once you recognize your anger cues, identify your choices of what you could do next. You could blow your top, scream, slam doors, or stomp out of the room. Or you could try to step back from the tenseness of the situation by taking several deep breaths while counting to ten. This relaxation technique can give you time to calm down and make a more thoughtful decision about what to do next.

Weigh the consequences of an angry, out-of-control response. If, for example, it had occurred to Philip that he would have been sent to the principal's office, he might have stopped himself from yelling at his teacher.

Take your mind off your anger. Relaxation techniques are helpful not only when trying to defuse a hostile situation but also when dealing with feelings of anger that last a long time. If you've been obsessing for days, weeks, or months over the wrongs someone did, make a conscious effort to turn your thoughts elsewhere. Use relaxation techniques while thinking about other things.

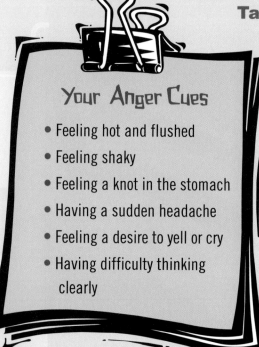

Your Anger Cues

- Feeling hot and flushed
- Feeling shaky
- Feeling a knot in the stomach
- Having a sudden headache
- Feeling a desire to yell or cry
- Having difficulty thinking clearly

Identify the Spark

The first rule for getting along with others is being able to recognize what makes you angry. If you can learn to recognize the spark that ignites your anger, you can figure out how to avoid situations where you may lose your temper.

The spark can be very minor. For example, every day your little brother annoys you while you're at the computer, doing homework. Instead of yelling at him, why not stop what you're doing and find out what he wants.

Try looking at things from a different point of view. Maybe your little brother is trying to get your attention because he likes you and wants to hang out with you. Perhaps you can make an effort to spend some time with him—tell him you'll spend some time with him if he leaves you alone until your homework is finished. Then, follow through, and suggest you both go outside and shoot some baskets. By changing the way you deal with your brother, you can change his behavior as well. Not only do you take care of your needs and his but you also avoid the spark that in the past would set off your anger.

Taking a step away from your problems may allow you to gain a new perspective. Other ways to take your mind off your anger include meditation and exercise. Or you might better spend your time playing or listening to music, drawing, or working on a favorite hobby. If you still need to focus on the issue itself, write about it in a journal or letter.

Sometimes it helps to get another person's perspective. Talk to a friend or your parents. And if you're ready to talk with the person you're feeling angry with, make sure you're ready to do so without your anger.

Learn to accept things you can't change. Even when you can figure out what's making you angry, sometimes you have to accept that there is nothing you can do about it. You can recognize that you don't like the situation, but you have to learn to live with it. Perhaps the school bus schedule was changed and now you have to wake up twenty minutes earlier. Or your parents are moving and you will be living hundreds of miles away from your best friend. Sometimes things are outside of your control.

Relax and listen to some of your favorite music to help alleviate tension and anger.

Getting angry over situations you can't change won't help. Recognize that life will be hard for a while, but you're resilient. Keep your sense of humor and look for the good in change. For example, the extra twenty minutes could give you time to finish up homework at school. Or perhaps your new home is

What You Should Do Next

Relax: Take deep breaths. With each breath focus on making your body relax. Count to ten slowly.

Problem solve: Think before you react: what might be the consequences of your actions?

Change the environment: Remove yourself from the situation so you can sort things out (leave the room or take a short walk). While you're gone, try to reduce your anger level by using relaxation exercises.

Communicate: After cooling down, talk to the other person if he or she is ready to talk. Speak in a quiet, calm voice as you talk out the problem. State your feelings in a polite, but assertive, way.

Remember: No one can "make you angry." You *decide* to become angry. How you express anger is your responsibility.

located just fifteen minutes away from your cousin's house so now you'll be able to spend more time hanging out with him. Looking for the positive aspects of change can be hard, but it can be a valuable way of coping with angry feelings.

CHAPTER NINE

When Others Are Out of Control

> *If you do that again I'm going to. . . .*
>
> *Oh, yeah?*
>
> *Well, make me. . . .*

What do you do when confronted by someone whose anger is out of control? Usually
the safest thing to do is to walk away, especially if you believe the
situation could become violent. Don't say anything at all to
provoke the other person. Insults and name-calling will quickly
make a bad situation worse.

**If you are confronted by someone who is looking for a fight, the safest
thing to do is to just walk away.**

When a Friend Is Angry

Stay upbeat and positive. Don't say anything to make the person angrier. Let your friend have his or her say without interrupting or being contradictory.

Know when to back off. If your friend needs time to cool down, give some space. Be sure you have a conversation later, when he or she is ready to talk calmly.

If you think your friend has a good reason to be angry, be supportive. If you think the anger is justified, it is okay to empathize (see the situation from his point of view). Help your friend figure out what to do to manage the anger.

Steer your friend away from destructive behavior. Make sure your friend knows you will prevent him or her from expressing anger by hurting others, vandalizing property, or hurting himself or herself. Talk to a parent or teacher if you are concerned that your friend might engage in destructive behavior.

However, if someone is doing something that you think is wrong, and you confront the person, be prepared to deal with a conflict. If it turns out that you are arguing with somebody who becomes threatening, don't respond to the threat. Be aware that your actions will influence what happens next. If you raise your voice, so will your opponent. If both of you become too angry to talk, then you need to move away from the situation.

If you think it is possible to talk about the problem, try to change the hostile tone. It can be hard to control yourself when

> "Anger is seldom without an argument but seldom with a good one."
>
> —Lord Halifax

someone is yelling at you. But do your best not to scream back. Don't try to impress any onlookers with how tough you can be. Instead, show them that you can be in control. Speak quietly and slowly, but remain firm. You can try to ease some of the tension by making a joke or by saying something like, "Let's work this out."

Have a conversation in which you listen to the other point of view. Make an effort to hear what the other person has to say and try to understand what is making the person angry. Don't be quick to dismiss his or her point of view as unreasonable. Keep your mind open. Be willing to accept the possibility that you might at least be partially to blame for the problem.

Seeing things your opponent's way can be an immense help in understanding his or her anger. In fact, it may also help make you feel less angry. Try to be empathetic. Put yourself in the other person's shoes and try to see the other side of the story.

Timing Is Everything

If you are trying to settle a problem, be sure to address the conflict when neither of you is rushed or upset. People are more irritable and less open to discussion and compromise if they are tired or frustrated. Any attempts to solve a conflict when both parties aren't ready to talk will most likely result in further problems.

Body Language and Anger

Sometimes, it is easy to tell when someone is angry even though the person denies it. He may raise his voice, or she may slam her books on a desk. An angry person's cheeks or face may turn red, usually as the result of a rise in blood pressure. A person's body language often speaks as clearly as his or her voice. An angry person often assumes a stiff posture and avoids eye contact.

You can also use body language to help calm down an angry person. During an argument, avoid using dramatic gestures, such as shaking your head, slamming your fists on the table, or waving your arms. Instead, try not to move at all—except for an occasional nod of the head to signal to your friend that you are listening and trying to understand the problem.

When the other person has finished speaking, ask questions. Try to find out why he or she is upset. Be sincere. Don't use a sarcastic tone, and avoid making accusations. You

Crossed arms and other body language can often tell you when someone is angry.

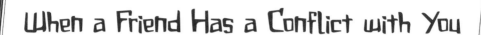

When a Friend Has a Conflict with You

- Allow him to have his say.
- Don't offer your opinion or make a judgment on what he has just said.
- Listen attentively and wait until your friend asks you to speak. That's a signal that he may have calmed down and is interested in resolving the argument.
- Explain your point of view.

need to convey the idea that you want to resolve the issue, not fan the flames.

For example, in trying to resolve a conflict with another guy, ask him what solution he would offer to the problem. Even if you don't agree with his solution, you may be able to reach a compromise. By getting the other person to put a proposed solution on the table, you have managed to open a dialogue that could lead to a resolution of the conflict. Even if you would have proposed the same solution, it may help defuse his anger if he thinks it's his idea.

It's okay to agree to disagree. What's important is that you are talking.

During your conversation, stick to the disagreement at hand and don't dredge up past issues. And don't make fun of the other person's feelings or point of view. Obviously, he feels very strongly about his position or he wouldn't be angry with you.

Try to keep the argument constructive. As both of you offer your respective viewpoints, see if you can find some common ground—places where you agree. See if you can boil the problem down to a few simple issues that are easily resolved. If you can see a way to resolve the issue, don't end the conversation until you both agree on the solution. Make sure the other person clearly understands what you intend to do to solve the problem. Likewise, you should understand what he intends to do to make sure the problem doesn't occur again.

Resolving Conflict Through Peer Mediation

Today, thousands of elementary, middle, and high schools across the nation make use of peer mediation programs to help students resolve disagreements that they can't resolve on their own. With peer mediation, students involved in a dispute take their problem to a neutral third party, or mediator. The mediator, who is also a student, listens to both sides, but doesn't decide who is right and who is wrong in a conflict. The two students involved are simply provided with a way to talk about their issue and asked to come up with their own solution to resolve it peacefully. Before participating in a peer mediation program, students must agree to abide by ground rules that include key elements of conflict resolution: tell the truth, listen without interrupting, and be respectful.

Taking a Stand

> One day, when Luis was in the convenience store, he was pulled aside by the store manager and told to leave. Luis didn't understand why. He explained that his mother had sent him to the store to buy milk. He even showed the manager the money. But the manager told Luis he had seen a boy steal candy from the counter then run out of the store. "The boy was a lot like you," the store manager said. "Now get out."
>
> Luis was angry. He realized that the manager meant the shoplifter was Hispanic, like Luis. And he knew that was not a good reason for the storeowner to prevent him from shopping there. He tried to talk to the manager to explain that he was there to shop. But the manager simply stated he didn't want any Hispanic kids in his store anymore.
>
> That night, Luis wrote a letter to the local newspaper explaining what happened to him. The day after the letter was published, members of a Hispanic rights group picketed the store. Within a few hours, the store manager had met with the leaders of the group and agreed to stop "racial profiling." He would no longer kick customers out of his store because of their ethnic background.

Anger is more than a reaction that helps the body protect itself. It also serves as a tool to motivate people to take action to solve problems or confront threats. Luis used his anger for positive purposes, responding in an assertive way in order to right a wrong.

Your anger can serve not only to motivate you, but also as a signal, making you aware that something is wrong. You can

When you believe something is wrong, your anger can give you the strength and determination to take a stand.

choose to respond to an event in an aggressive way—for instance, Luis could have decided to vandalize the store. Or you can respond in a healthy, assertive, and respectful way, as Luis did, by using anger to identify a problem and try to fix it. Your anger can help you stand up for what you believe in.

Over the decades, laws have been passed and elections have been won because people have been angry about injustices. Demonstrators, protestors, and voters have used their anger to take action and work to bring about change.

"Our lives begin to end the day we become silent about things that matter."

—Martin Luther King, Jr.

Anger can give you the determination to be assertive. Anger can help individuals as well. It can give the victims of a bully the energy and motivation to finally take a stand against the person terrorizing them. It can help someone act to stop another person from being bullied. It can provide the drive to someone with an addiction to break that addiction by making changes in his or her life. Anger helps provide the energy to act or do something differently when in an uncomfortable or unfair situation.

Most experts agree that when anger is part of a conflict with another person, the best way to respond is by being assertive. That is, you need to clearly communicate what you are thinking and what you expect from the other person. But being assertive also means that you express yourself calmly and respectfully.

Can Anger Be Bad for Your Health?

Studies have shown that people who don't express anger in good ways can harm their health. Those who are passive and keep their anger bottled up and those who aggressively vent their anger are more prone to headaches, sleeping disorders, high blood pressure, or digestive problems. Some studies show that stress and hostility related to stress are linked to heart attacks.[1] Other research indicates that chronically angry persons are more susceptible to pain.[2]

When you learn how to express anger appropriately, you'll be helping to keep yourself in the best of health.

Anger over discrimination against African Americans motivated Dr. Martin Luther King, Jr. to begin a peaceful movement with the goal of obtaining equal rights for all Americans, no matter the color of their skin.

Learn how to use anger wisely. During the teen years, you will be faced with many issues, including questions of identity, separation from parents, and relationships with others. It is likely you will feel angry at times. Learning how to deal with this anger in a positive way is a necessary part of growing up.

Anger is a complicated emotion. When it erupts out of control, it can lead to bitter arguments, hard feelings, and even violence. But when it is properly managed, it can serve as a healthy release of tension, a way for you to grow emotionally, and a tool to help bring about change.

CHAPTER NOTES

Chapter 1. What Is Anger?

1. Carroll E. Izard, *The Psychology of Emotions* (New York: Plenum Press, 1991), p. 248.

2. Quoted in Nicole Walker, "Why Anger Is Bad for Your Health," *Jet*, May 1, 2000, p. 16.

3. Clayton E. Tucker-Ladd, "Chapter 7: Anger and Aggression," *Psychological Self-Help*, <http://www.psychologicalselfhelp.org> (July 15, 2007).

4. Ibid.

Chapter 2. Are You Quick to Anger?

1. "Artest Timeline: Ron-Ron's Troubled Past," *ESPN.com*, March 27, 2007, <http://sports.espn.go.com/nba/news/story?id=2281289> (July 15, 2007).

2. William Pollack, "What Makes Boys Violent? We Do," *USA Weekend.com*, April 16, 2000, <http://www.usaweekend.com/00_issues/000416/000416boys.html> (July 15, 2007).

Chapter 4. When You're Angry with Friends

1. James V. O'Connor, "Why Are We So #!&*@ Mad?" *USA Today Magazine*, September 2000, p. 56.

2. American Psychological Association News Release, "Catharsis Increases Rather Than Decreases Anger and Aggression, According to a New Study." *APA Online*, March 5, 1999. <http://www.apa.org/releases/catharsis.html> (July 15, 2007).

3. O'Connor, p. 56.

Chapter 6. I'm Not Taking It Anymore!

1. Adapted from Dorothea M. Ross, *Childhood Bullying and Teasing: What School Personnel, Other Professionals, and Parents Can Do* (Alexandria, Va.: American Counseling Association, 2003), p. 93.

2. Nemours Foundation, "Helping Kids Deal with Bullies," *KidsHealth*, June 2007, <http://www.kidshealth.org/parent/emotions/behavior/bullies.html> (July 15, 2007).

Chapter 7. Bottled-Up Anger

1. U.S. Centers for Disease Control and Prevention, "Suicide: Facts at a Glance," Summer 2007, <http://www.cdc.gov/ncipc/dvp/suicide/SuicideDataSheet.pdf> (July 15, 2007).

Chapter 10. Taking a Stand

1. Mayo Clinic Staff. "Anger Management FAQ: The Good, the Bad, the Ugly," *MayoClinic.com*, June 26, 2007, <http://www.mayoclinic.com/health/anger-management/MH00075> (July 15, 2007).

2. Stephen Bruehl, Ok Chung, and John W. Burns, "Anger Expression and Pain: An Overview of Findings and Possible Mechanisms," *Journal of Behavioral Medicine*, June 29, 2006, pp. 593–606.

adrenaline—A hormone secreted from the adrenal glands when the body is under stress.

aggression—Hostile or violent behavior.

anger—A strong emotion characterized by annoyance or displeasure.

anxiety—A feeling of uneasiness, usually over something that is about to happen.

assertive—Able to express one's own needs and wishes while respecting those of others.

conflict—A struggle that results from disagreements about needs, wishes, demands, or opinions.

cortisol—A hormone associated with anger and fear that is produced by the adrenal glands.

depression—Long-lasting feelings of sadness and hopelessness and a loss of interest in life.

emotion—A state of mind that is a reaction to an outside event. Some emotions include anger, joy, guilt, or other feelings.

fight-or-flight instinct—The initial reaction of the body when a person feels threatened.

frustration—A feeling of being upset or annoyed resulting from the failure to change something or achieve a desired goal.

hormone—A substance produced by the cells of the body that influences behavior and mood.

passive-aggressive—Not openly showing hostility, but behaving in a way that shows the person resents and is increasingly angry toward someone else.

psychiatrist—Medical doctor who specializes in treating mental illnesses.

psychologist—An expert in the study of the human mind and behavior.

self-esteem—Respect for oneself.

stress—Physical and emotional strain caused by external forces or circumstances.

FURTHER READING

Maxym, Carol, and Leslie B. York. *Teens in Turmoil: A Path to Change for Parents, Adolescents and Their Families*. New York: Penguin Books, 2000.

Scheunemann, Pam. *Coping with Anger*. Edina, Minn.: Abdo Publishing, 2004.

Seaward, Brian, and Linda Bartlett. *Hot Stones and Funny Bones: Teens Helping Teens Cope with Stress and Anger*. Deerfield Beach, Fla.: HCI Teens, 2002.

Wilde, Jerry. *More Hot Stuff to Help Kids Chill Out: The Anger and Stress Management Book*. Richmond, Ind.: LGR Publishing, 2001.

INTERNET ADDRESSES

American Psychological Association: Controlling Anger—Before It Controls You

http://www.apa.org/topics/controlanger.html

BAM! or Body and Mind Guide to Getting Along

http://www.bam.gov/sub_yourlife/yourlife_conflict.html

It's My Life

http://pbskids.org/itsmylife/emotions/anger/index.html

HOTLINE TELEPHONE NUMBERS

National Domestic Violence Hotline

1-800-799-SAFE (1-800-799-7233)

National Suicide Prevention Lifeline

1-800-273-TALK (1-800-273-8255)

CONTRIBUTORS

Author **Hal Marcovitz** lives in Pennsylvania, with his wife, Gail Snyder, who is a coauthor of this book, and their daughters. He has written more than 90 books for young readers. His other titles in the Flip-It-Over Guides to Teen Emotions series are *A Guys' Guide to Jealousy* and *A Guys' Guide to Loneliness*.

Series advisor **Dr. Carroll Izard** is the Trustees Distinguished Professor of Psychology at the University of Delaware. His research and writing focuses on the development of emotion knowledge and emotion regulation and their contributions to social and emotional competence. He is author or editor of seventeen books (one of which won a national award) and more than one hundred articles in scientific journals. Dr. Izard is a fellow of both national psychological associations and the American Association for the Advancement of Science. He is the winner of the American Psychological Association's G. Stanley Hall Award and an international exchange fellowship from the National Academy of Sciences.

FLIP-IT-OVER GUIDES TO TEEN EMOTIONS

A Guys' Guide to Anger; A Girls' Guide to Anger
ISBN-13: 978-0-7660-2853-1   ISBN-10: 0-7660-2853-4

A Guys' Guide to Conflict; A Girls' Guide to Conflict
ISBN-13: 978-0-7660-2852-4   ISBN-10: 0-7660-2852-6

A Guys' Guide to Jealousy; A Girls' Guide to Jealousy
ISBN-13: 978-0-7660-2854-8   ISBN-10: 0-7660-2854-2

A Guys' Guide to Loneliness; A Girls' Guide to Loneliness
ISBN-13: 978-0-7660-2856-2   ISBN-10: 0-7660-2856-9

A Guys' Guide to Love; A Girls' Guide to Love
ISBN-13: 978-0-7660-2855-5   ISBN-10: 0-7660-2855-0

A Guys' Guide to Stress; A Girls' Guide to Stress
ISBN-13: 978-0-7660-2857-9   ISBN-10: 0-7660-2857-7

STOP

**Boring Guys' Stuff
From This Point On!**

GIRLS!

FLIP-iT-OVER
GUIDES TO TEEN EMOTIONS

A Girls' Guide to

Anger

Gail Snyder

Enslow Publishers, Inc.
40 Industrial Road
Box 398
Berkeley Heights, NJ 07922
USA

http://www.enslow.com

Library of Congress Cataloging-in-Publication Data

Marcovitz, Hal.
  A guys' guide to anger ; A girls' guide to anger / Hal Marcovitz and Gail Snyder.
      p. cm. — (Flip-it-over guides to teen emotions)
  Includes bibliographical references and index.
  ISBN-13: 978-0-7660-2853-1
  ISBN-10: 0-7660-2853-4
  1. Anger—Juvenile literature. 2. Boys—Life skills guides—Juvenile literature. 3. Girls—Life skills guides—Juvenile literature. I. Snyder, Gail. II. Title. III. Title: Guys' guide to anger ; A girls' guide to anger. IV. Title: Girls' guide to anger.
  BF575.A5M33 2008
  155.42'4247—dc22
                                           2007026459
Printed in the United States of America.
112009 Lake Book Manufacturing, Inc., Melrose Park, IL

10 9 8 7 6 5 4 3 2

Produced by OTTN Publishing, Stockton, N.J.

To Our Readers: We have done our best to make sure all Internet Addresses in this book were active and appropriate when we went to press. However, the author and the publisher have no control over and assume no liability for the material available on those Internet sites or on other Web sites they may link to. Any comments or suggestions can be sent by e-mail to comments@enslow.com or to the address on the title page.

Photo Credits: © iStockphoto.com/Fred Goldstein, 1, 34; © iStockphoto.com/Paul Kline, 33; Used under license from Shutterstock, Inc., 3, 4, 6, 7, 10, 12, 13, 15, 18, 22, 24, 27, 28, 30, 31, 35, 36, 38, 40, 42, 44, 46, 48, 50, 53, 54, 56.

Cover Photo: © iStockphoto.com/Fred Goldstein.

CONTENTS

I'm So Mad...

> I couldn't believe it when my mother told me that I couldn't go to Kelsey's party. I had been looking forward to it for weeks. Mom told me I had stay home just because I had gotten another bad report card. I tried to tell her how unfair it was, but she wouldn't listen to me.
>
> I ran upstairs to my room and slammed the door so hard it cracked. Then I scooped up a sculpture of a dog I made that my mother really liked and hurled it to the floor. It broke into a million satisfying pieces. I was standing in the middle of the room with my heart pounding and my hands curled into fists. All I could think was, what else could I throw?
>
> —Jenna

Jenna was experiencing all of the physical symptoms of having kicked into anger mode. Her heart was racing, her body was stiff, and she couldn't think clearly.

Whenever you are angry, your body automatically reacts the same way, regardless of the

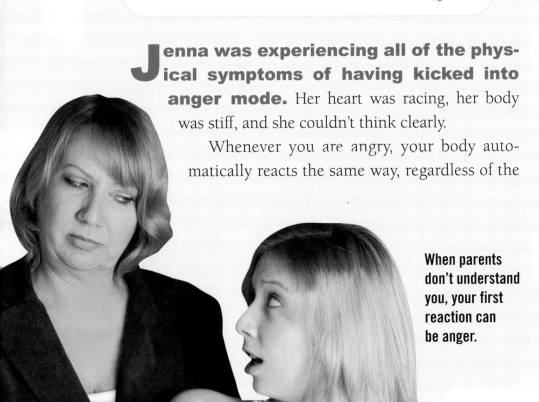

When parents don't understand you, your first reaction can be anger.

You and Your Emotions

A part of everyone's personality, emotions are a powerful driving force in life. They are hard to define and understand. But what is known is that emotions—which include anger, fear, love, joy, jealousy, and hate—are a normal part of the human system. They are responses to situations and events that trigger bodily changes, motivating you to take some kind of action.

Some studies show that the brain relies more on emotions than on intellect in learning and in making decisions. Being able to identify and understand the emotions in yourself and in others can help you in your relationships with family, friends, and others throughout your life.

situation. Your muscles get tense and your heart starts to beat faster. These changes in your body mean you are physically ready to respond to the threat before you.

This response is known as the "fight-or-flight" instinct. It has been part of being human since prehistoric times, when people needed to deal with wild animals and other dangers. The instinct allows the body to prepare to stand and confront a threat or to run away.

This fight-or-flight instinct is an automatic response that helps protect you from harm. But it also occurs when there isn't any actual physical danger—only the feeling of needing to protect yourself from some kind of threat or danger. The same response happens whether a speeding car is hurtling toward you, or you hear a particularly nasty insult from a boy you can't stand. This protective instinct causes your

Fight-or-Flight Emotions

The fight-or-flight instinct typically involves the basic emotions of both fear and anger. Anger (like any other emotion) rarely exists for very long before another emotion or two come into play. If you can identify the pattern of emotions you are feeling, you are on your way to being able to take charge of them.

body to respond whenever you feel irritated, disrespected, shamed, or embarrassed by others.

Lots of things can make you angry. Sometimes the unfairness of events in your life may seem overwhelming. It may be that one of your friends kissed the boy you've had a crush on, or a girl is spreading rumors about you at school. Or perhaps you believe that your parents are being unfair because they give your brother more freedom than you have. In all of these cases you can experience various emotions, along with anger.

You may be having a lot of trouble dealing with your emotions these days. This is especially true if you are going through the physical changes of puberty—the stage when your body is maturing into that of an adult. Controlling your emotions during puberty can be especially hard. That's because the emotional center

One way to get a grip on your anger is to figure out how other emotions, such as fear or disappointment, might be fueling angry feelings.

of the brain—the amygdala—is in charge. As you grow older, the part of the brain that handles reasoning and judgment—the pre-frontal cortex—will be in control. So while the amygdala is running the show, you can experience emotional highs and lows that make you feel like you're out of control. During this time in your life, even little things may set you off and make you feel mad.

Your changing moods are also affected by special chemical substances in your body called hormones. During

What Happens When You're Angry?

A red face

Dilated pupils

Tears

Dry mouth

Feeling flushed

A knot in the stomach

Rapid breathing

puberty, the levels of hormones in a girl's body, especially estrogen and progesterone, keep changing. These hormones affect behavior and mood. So when the levels of hormones in your body keep changing, your moods can change, too. You are also more likely to get angry because nobody seems to understand you.

Just feeling sad or stressed out can make you grouchy and angry over things that may not normally bother you at all. For example, if your life is going smoothly, a bad grade on your math test may upset you a little, but you'll just resolve to study harder next time. However, if that same test

Degrees of Anger

The word anger describes emotions that cover a wide range. When you are angry, you may be mildly annoyed, somewhat irritated, rather mad, simply outraged, or incredibly furious.

result happens after you've been grounded for staying out too late, you are likely to get angry and upset. If you are tired or not feeling well, you may also be more likely to take offense or get angry.

How you express your anger. How do you act when you're angry? Some people physically and verbally lash out. They yell at or hit others, break things, or act mean. They're expressing anger by being aggressive—that is, by acting in hostile or violent ways. Being aggressive with others seldom solves any issues. In fact, it often leads to more problems because it makes the person on the receiving end angry, too.

Expressing Anger

There are big differences in the way girls and boys express anger, says author Rachel Simmons.[1] American society tends to expect boys to directly show anger—with words or physically, although only if they don't seriously hurt anyone. However, girls are often taught that expressing their anger this way is bad.

As a result, if a girlfriend is angry at you, it is likely that she won't come out and tell you so. You may have to figure it out by the clues she leaves. She may tease you about something she's never brought up before, stop talking to you, or tell stories about you that aren't true. But what she may not do is tell you what made her angry or give you a chance to make it up to her.

However, it is possible to express your anger in ways that don't harm others. You are taking charge of your anger when you communicate your feelings in healthy ways—that is, by being honest and up-front, but not hurtful. This way of talking with friends, parents, teachers, and other people in your life can help you improve your relationships with them.

For example, Elise and Jamie have been friends for a long time. But Jamie has a habit that has been getting on Elise's nerves. Whenever Elise asks Jamie for her opinion, Jamie doesn't give one. She usually replies, "I don't care—whatever you want." Jamie's laid-back attitude had really been bothering Elise lately, and she finally decided to say something about it. Although she was feeling angry, she spoke calmly as she explained her frustration with Jamie. Although Jamie felt surprised at first, she appreciated her friend's honesty, and she promised to make some changes. Both girls felt better about their friendship.

Getting a grip on your anger is important. Are you quick to anger? Do you break things when you get mad? Have you ever hurt anyone when you were angry? Did you feel bad about it afterwards? Do you believe you are having trouble dealing with

You can feel angry when stressed out over too many tests and too much homework.

The Surveys Say...

In a national poll, Harvard University researchers surveyed more than 1,500 middle and high school students about their anger. One third admitted that they had trouble controlling their anger. Twenty-one percent of the girls said they had gotten into fights because they had been insulted, disrespected, or involved in an ongoing disagreement. More than twice the number of boys made the same admission.[2]

people because you can't manage angry feelings? If you answered yes to any of these questions, then you need some help dealing with your anger and learning better ways to express your feelings.

Just remember, feeling angry is normal. It is the actions you take as a result of your anger that can solve conflicts and problems, or make them worse. Anger can be a real problem in your life if you let it. But learning to manage your anger will not only improve your relationships with others, but also help make you feel better about yourself. By practicing some of the ideas and tips in this book, you will understand this powerful emotion and have the tools to handle anger in yourself as well as in others.

When you get angry, you have choices: you can choose to stay angry or you can calm down and think about how to resolve your issues.

How Do You Show Anger?

One day at school Angela and Erica were talking between classes. Suddenly Felice burst in on their conversation. Shoving Erica hard against the lockers, Felice angrily accused the younger girl of flirting with her boyfriend. Angela knew Felice was just being a bully and that the claim wasn't true. So she was shocked to hear Erica quickly apologize and say it wouldn't happen again. Angela was angry for her friend. She turned to Felice and in a cool, firm voice told her to leave Erica alone.

Different people will often react to the same incident in different ways. One person step backs and claims not to be bothered, another person is inspired to take some kind of action, and a third person becomes furious. Are you like that third person? Do you tend to get angry often? Take the quiz on pages 14 and 15 to find out.

Your answers to the quiz may depend on your personality. In general, if you have an aggressive personality, you tend to get angry easily—and show that anger—more often than people who

Aggressive people have no problems broadcasting their anger.

are assertive or passive. So what exactly are these different kinds of personalities?

Aggressive. People who have aggressive personalities usually don't give much thought to other people's feelings because they typically put their needs ahead of anyone else's. They often seem to think they know best and are better than other people. When something goes wrong, they find someone else to blame rather than themselves. Quick to anger, aggressive personalities often number among the bullies at school. They're also the people most likely to get sent to the principal's office for talking back to teachers or getting into fights. Using threats to get what they want, aggressive people are often feared by their classmates, but are typically not well liked or admired.

Passive. People with a passive personalities tend to fear confrontations. When faced with a situation that would make most people mad, they often don't look angry. There is no red face, clenched fists, or heavy breathing. Because they simply want the uncomfortable situation to go away, they deal with it—and most confrontations—by giving in. They will assume blame for a problem, even when they are innocent, and often place other people's needs ahead of their own. They don't attempt to seek revenge, but they don't try to suggest a fair and proper solution to the problem, either. Some passive people act that way because they don't value themselves—they suffer from low self-esteem.

Passive people tend to react to stressful situations by hoping they'll go away.

Rate Yourself:
Do You Get Angry Easily?

Do you agree with the following statements? Give yourself three points if your answer is "often," two points if it is "some of the time," one point if "rarely," and zero points for "never."

1. If my friend cancels on me at the last minute, I get mad at her.

2. I hate waiting in line.

3. When someone disagrees with me, I make sure they know they are wrong.

4. When I get mad, I throw, hit, or break things.

5. I get angry at myself when I do something wrong or badly.

6. When someone treats me poorly, I think about ways that I can get back at them.

7. I've gotten in trouble at school because of my anger.

8. I have been so angry that I have pushed, kicked, or slapped another person.

9. Other people have told me that I get angry too much or that I am scary when I get mad.

10. I curse at people when I get mad and try to make them feel bad.

11. Sometimes I don't feel like I'm in control of my anger.

12. I am easily offended by comments people make about me and can't stop thinking about them.

13. I frequently feel bad about things I have said or done while I was mad.

14. When I dislike someone I let them know.

15. When I don't get my way I get very upset.

Add up the numbers: 0–8 points means you're pretty good at handling situations that make people angry. Anger sometimes causes problems in your life if your score is 9–20. More than 20 points indicates that you probably get angry easily—and that you need to find better ways to handle your anger.[1]

Science Says....

James Averill, author of the book *Anger and Aggression*, says most people experience anger several times a week. Some people become angry several times each day. Yet Averill's research shows that only 10 percent of the time does this anger result in someone physically hurting another person. In fact, he found that 19 percent of the time the angry persons funneled their emotions into being "extra nice."[2] In other words, they behaved in a passive way, by not directly dealing with the situation by standing up for themselves.

Assertive. People with assertive personalities try to understand and support everyone's rights. Because they tend to have high self-esteem, they believe other people are not necessarily out to hurt or take advantage of them. Their high self-esteem means they can listen to criticism and consider its merits. They respond to disagreements without taking offense or thinking they are stupid or worthless. When an assertive person is faced with a situation that could cause anger, he or she thinks about the best way to resolve the problem before acting.

A complex combination. Of course, it is possible that you can see yourself in some of the descriptions of each of these personality types. Most people don't fall neatly into a single category. Depending on the situation and the people involved, you may act in a different way. For instance, at home you might demonstrate passive behavior with your parents, while at school, you may be assertive with your classmates and friends.

However, you will find that in most cases, when you act assertive, you will have the best results in dealing with others.

When you are assertive, you are able to honestly communicate your feelings. Although that doesn't guarantee you will always get what you want, you will feel better when you can honestly share things with friends, family members, and other important people in your life. And by talking about your emotions, you will prevent them from staying bottled up inside of you—which can cause even more problems. By being assertive, you will let others know how they can better consider your feelings in the future.

Learned behaviors. Your temperament and personality aren't the only influences on how you experience and express feelings of anger—and other emotions for that matter. Over the years, you may have learned certain ways of dealing with anger based on how your parents or friends behaved in stressful situations. If your parents yelled and hollered when they were angry, it's likely you do the same thing, too. Some scientists report that teens who respond with violence when they are angry do so because they were exposed to it while growing up—either by witnessing it or being the victim of it.[3] Even if you've learned some unhealthy ways of expressing anger, you can unlearn those behaviors.

Anger As a Way of Life?

People who anger easily often have a set pattern of beliefs, attitudes, and expectations of themselves and of others. They often believe that their way is the only way to do things, and feel threatened when others question their actions.

When Friends Make You Mad

Kaitlyn sat on the step of her porch, stewing over what just happened. Mackenzie had actually broken up her party by inviting everyone over to her house. "We'll be back in an hour or so," she said. "But you should probably hang around until your other guests come." It was now three hours later and no one else had arrived. Maybe they were at Mackenzie's house, too. Kaitlyn was furious at her so-called friend and wondered why she had invited her in the first place.

You can have the best time of your life when with friends. They can make you feel understood, respected, and a part of something. But you can be

When you're upset with your friend, don't share your feelings by yelling at her. Talk to her calmly and listen to what she has to say.

devastated by friends, too, when they disappoint you, hurt your feelings, or make you angry.

There are many ways that friends can upset you. You may be angry over something a girl-friend said or did. Or you can be disappointed to learn she didn't tell you the truth. Perhaps your team lost the big game, and you think one of your teammates didn't make her best effort. Or you're upset that your party was a bust because one the girls you invited was rude, and your friends went home early. Maybe one of your friends got caught talking in class, and the teacher decided to keep everyone after school.

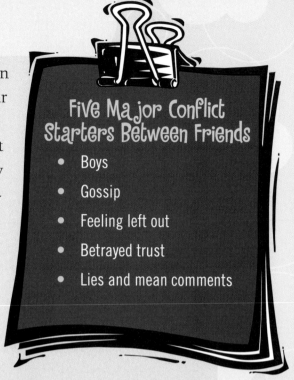

Five Major Conflict Starters Between Friends

- Boys
- Gossip
- Feeling left out
- Betrayed trust
- Lies and mean comments

Researchers have found that when girls are angry, they tend not to be honest with each other. They are hesitant to confront one another and say what they are feeling. Instead, they often stop talking altogether, and give each other the silent treatment. If girls would talk frankly with each other, professor of psychology Sharon Lamb says, they would probably find ways to resolve their differences. "In all relationships, if you get angry with people, you talk it out," she says.[1]

Talk to each other. If you want to keep your friend-ship, there are steps you can take to mend an argument:

- Make the first move. Don't let your anger grow. By tak-ing the first step, you're showing your friend how important your friendship is to you. At this point you

don't need to apologize or admit fault. Make it clear that you want to talk.

- Be prepared about what you want to say. Think about the points you want to make. It may help to write them down ahead of time.

- Be prepared to listen. At the beginning of your conversation, establish a rule that neither of you is to interrupt the other. Then, be sure to listen—don't think about what you're going to say next. Pay attention to what your friend is saying.

- Try to empathize with your friend. That is, try to see and understand her point of view.

Accept responsibility if you are at fault. If you discover that you have wronged the other person, sincerely apologize for what you have done. If you receive an apology from the other person, graciously accept it and do your best to forgive her and put the incident behind you.

When speaking with the other person, it helps to use statements that begin with the word "I" and not the word "You." I-messages allow you to clearly state your feelings. In a calm voice, state what is bothering you, why it bothers you, and what you think

A True Apology Should Be Given:

- With sincerity
- With a genuine understanding of the issue
- Without any conditions
- Without the expectation of an apology in return

Use "I," Not "You"

I-messages allow you to tell someone how you feel without placing blame on the person involved with a conflict. I-messages focus on how the problem affects you and what you would like to see happen to fix things. It has four basic parts:

"I feel..." (States the emotions you are feeling.)

"...when..." (Gives details about what the other person did or said that caused the hard feelings.)

"...because..." (Explains why you feel that way. This can be the hardest part of the I-message.)

"I want..." (Describes what you think will resolve the conflict or ease the bad feelings.)

ought to be done about it. Don't expect anyone to know what you are thinking unless you tell him or her.

When a friend is angry with you. There may be times when a friend acts angry with you for no clear reason. Before you get angry in return, stop and consider what might be making him or her irritable. Do you sometimes find yourself in a negative mood, when nothing seems to be going right? Maybe your friend is not acting like him- or herself for the same reason. Recognize that if a friend is saying or doing negative things, it may be because he or she is feeling bad about something. Rather than take harsh words too personally, give your friend a day or two. Then see if he or she wants to talk. By trying to understand

When you're angry with a friend, write down a list of reasons why, and explain how her actions affected you. This will help you focus on what to say when you talk with her.

Anger

When a Friend Is Angry

Stay upbeat and positive. Don't say anything to make the person angrier. Let your friend have his or her say without interrupting.

Know when to back off. If your friend needs time to cool down, give her some space. Be sure you have a conversation later, when he or she is ready to talk calmly.

If you think your friend's anger is justified, show some empathy. When he or she is ready to talk, discuss ways to deal with the issue and manage that anger.

Steer him or her away from destructive behavior. Let your friend know you will stop her from harming others or himself or herself. Talk to a parent or teacher if you are concerned that your friend might engage in destructive behavior.

what's going on in your friend's heart and mind, you don't make the situation worse by yelling or retaliating in some other way.

When dealing with angry confrontations, do your best to keep lines of communication open. Rather than expressing your anger by giving your friend the silent treatment, keep talking until you find a solution to your problem.

"Holding on to anger, resentment and hurt only gives you tense muscles, a headache and a sore jaw from clenching your teeth."
—Joan Lunden

Feeling Angry with Siblings

Eleven-year-old Allison is four years younger than her sister Amber. When their parents go out, Amber is often asked to baby-sit Allison. But Allison hates it when her older sister is in charge. Amber orders her around, and curses at her and calls her names as soon as their parents leave the house.

If you have a sister and you seem to always be fighting with her, you are not alone. Most sisters—and brothers—are often at odds. But conflicts can become serious problems when kids express anger with verbal abuse or physical violence. There are several different ways that Allison can respond to her sister's aggressive behavior. Which do you think will have the best results?

Allison and Amber have an angry relationship that Allison wants to work on.

Don't say anything at all. This passive approach will do nothing to stop Amber's behavior. In addition, if Amber continues to treat her younger sister this way, the relationship between the two of them will remain hostile. In addition, by holding her feelings in, Allison runs the risk of reaching a breaking point and reacts with violence. This is definitely not a good solution.

Skills Needed to Work Out Conflicts

- Being respectful
- Being understanding
- Being assertive

Yell and scream back at Amber. Although Allison may think she feels better by venting, she is making a bad situation worse. Name-calling and harsh words tend to make the other person in a conflict even angrier than she was before. And again, it can lead to violence.

Walk away from the situation at first and wait until she feels calmer. When Allison's over her stormy feelings, she should try to have a conversation with Amber to see if there is a specific issue that set off her sister's anger. It is important that she confront Amber, saying something like, "We need to talk this through." She needs to be assertive—to stand her ground and tell Amber to stop. If this last approach doesn't work,

Feeling angry—no matter what the cause—is never an excuse for violence or abuse.

"He who angers you, conquers you."

-Elizabeth Kenny

Allison needs to bring her parents into the picture. They should know what's going on. **Conflicts among sisters and brothers are normal.** Family members bicker and have arguments with one another for the same reasons they argue with other people. Both want the other person to see things from his or her own point of view.

Many siblings fight because of jealousy. A sister may become very angry if she believes her parents are playing favorites. Or a girl may complain that her parents are not being fair because she and her brother have to abide by different family rules and curfews. Relationships among brothers and sisters are usually most strained when siblings are of the same gender and near one another in age.

Conflicts between siblings also occur when they don't respect each other's property. For instance, suppose you are angry with your sister because she wore your favorite jeans without your permission. To make matters worse, when she was done with them, she dropped them inside out on the floor of her room. You could complain loudly, "You always borrow my stuff without asking me and never return it to its proper place!" However, you-statements with words like "always" and "never" are likely to make your sister defensive. She'll probably hurl an accusation of her own right back at you.

Manage your conflicts. If you really want to solve the conflict and prevent it from happening again, you need to use some conflict management techniques. Your sister will be

less inclined to take offense if you use an I-message to explain why you're angry: "I'm upset because you borrowed my jeans without asking me. They are my favorite pair and I saved a long time before I was able to buy them." Be sure to follow up with a sentence explaining how you'd like things to go in the future: "Next time, please ask my permission before you go in my closet."

Know when to ask for help. Sometimes hard feelings can't be resolved on your own. If you have tried to work things out with your sister without success, or if you and your brother keep fighting, you need to talk to your parents. When you tell your side of the story, try to keep your voice calm and use I-messages to describe your feelings. Don't attack your sibling with words or fists. It is important that your parents understand your feelings of anger. And they will be impressed to see that you know how to manage conflict in the family in a mature way.

Sometimes disagreements between siblings may need a parent's intervention.

Keeping Your Cool with Adults

Lindsey loved basketball. However, she knew that her parents didn't approve of girls playing sports. Although she wanted to try out for the basketball team in seventh grade, Lindsey did not dare oppose her parent's wishes. Instead, she joined the debate club, because it was an activity that her mother and father thought to be more suitable for a girl.

Lindsey didn't tell her parents about how much she wanted to play basketball. But she felt angry at them for refusing to allow her to go out for the team. That anger did not go away. Instead, it resurfaced every time she argued with her parents about other things.

Lindsey was angry with her parents, but didn't know how to express her feelings. All she knew was that her parents didn't understand what was important to her. And she didn't feel like she could talk to them or change their way of thinking.

Part of growing up involves breaking away from your parents, as you begin to want to think for yourself and make your own decisions. From time to time, you will probably get angry when you have differences of opinion with your mother, father, or other adult family members. If you are

upset about a parental rule that you think is unfair or babyish, you need to let your mother and father know how you feel.

However, the way that you express your opinion is important. Yelling, breaking things, or storming off to your room won't get you very far. A more effective solution would be to wait until you are no longer upset. Then, approach your parents and in a quiet voice ask to talk further. During your discussion, stay calm and use logical arguments to explain your side.

Family stresses. The same holds true when you're angry about other issues. Family changes and other stresses such as divorce, unemployment, money problems, abuse, illness, or impending moves can increase feelings of anger and tension in households. The best way to deal with your feelings is to try to talk with the adults in your life about how you are affected by what's going on. If you express your anger by refusing to talk to others, you won't change anything. And you won't feel very good about yourself, either.

Anger in the Family

Every family is different in the way its members handle anger. Kids often learn from what they experience at home. If your mom and dad yell at you a lot or even at each other, you are likely to express your anger in the same manner.

However, be aware that this method of dealing with your anger isn't likely to produce good results. It is important to remember that you have a choice on how you respond when you are angry. It is up to you to decide how you will act—being aggressive or being calm and assertive.

If your parents are angry with you, try to step back from arguing with them. Stop and think about where your parents may be coming from. They may be having a hard time with work, with an ill family member, or some other stressful situation. As a result they may not be thinking clearly. They may even be taking their anger out on you.

In dealing with an angry parent, don't try to explain your side of the story right away. Instead, wait for a while until your mom or dad has calmed down. Then, in a respectful voice, use an I-message to explain where you are coming from. If you feel your mother or father is unable to connect with you, you may want to talk to another trusted adult or to a school counselor.

Dealing with other adults. Your parents probably aren't the only adults who may make you angry sometimes. For example, you may believe that some of your teachers are treating you unfairly or letting some students in your class get away with breaking rules while coming down hard on you. In some cases, you may also believe that teachers are favoring certain students over others.

Some students complain that their teachers get mad and yell too much at their students, sometimes singling out a kid in front of the whole class. Rather than simply complaining among themselves about a teacher's actions, students might feel better if they made the effort to point out the problem. After all, it is possible that a teacher is not aware she's upset a student who thinks she's picking on him, or that her kids think she is playing favorites.

If you are angry with your teacher, don't try to talk in the heat of your anger. Take some time to settle down and think about what you can do. If you think you can discuss your problem calmly, you should try to have a conversation with your teacher so you can let him or her know your problem. Be courteous and polite. Don't confront the teacher and put him or her on the defensive by making wild accusations.

Talking with your
teacher is the best way
to fix a problem.

Tips on Talking to Parents and Other Adults

Bring up your issue when the adult has the time to listen. Don't try to talk to your parents when they're busy with something or someone else or rushing out the door. Say, "Is this a good time for you? I have something important to discuss."

Be aware of your body language. Don't roll your eyes, cross your arms, or clench your fists. Look the other person in the eyes and try to remain calm.

Use respectful language. Don't use sarcasm, insults, or put-downs when explaining your point of view. Snapping something like, "That's a stupid reason," will only make the other person angrier.

Be honest. Tell the truth about how you feel or what has happened; your parents and other adults want to trust you.

Listen to the other side of the issue. The adult will be more likely to show you the same respect.

State your case using "I-messages." "I feel pressured because I need to get this report done tonight so I don't really have time walk the dog," or "I don't agree because . . . ."

If you are not happy with the outcome, you should take your concerns home with you and share them with your parents. Tell them what's been happening in class and answer any questions

Before trying to have a serious conversation with your mother, make sure she has time to listen.

they may have. Simply taking this step may actually help you feel better right away, especially if your parents are sympathetic to your story. Their next step may be to go to school and have a meeting with your teacher and school administrator. In most cases, a parent-teacher meeting will make things better for everyone.

If you are afraid to talk to your parents about your problem, you can approach your school guidance counselor instead. Talking things out with another adult can help you focus on exactly what is going on in your head and in the teacher's. You may discover options you had not thought about.

When You Keep Anger Inside

Carol was having terrible headaches and stomachaches. Her worried mother took her to the doctor, who was unable to find a medical cause for the symptoms. He then referred Carol and her mother to a therapist—someone who treats people with relationship problems. After working with the family therapist for a while, Carol finally opened up to him. She mentioned that her mother had just begun a job with evening hours. Carol's headaches and stomachaches always occurred on school nights, when she was home alone.

Carol was angry about a lot of things, but she couldn't express her anger. Her parents had just divorced, and she was angry about the breakup. She had moved to a new school and was angry about losing her best friend. And she was angry that her mother's new job hours meant Carol was left alone in the evening. However, Carol didn't acknowledge any of that anger. She figured her mother had

Carol was having headaches because she wasn't dealing with her anger properly.

It's Hard to Ignore Anger

Anger is like an inflatable beach ball that you can't really push completely underwater. It keeps popping back up at you, no matter how hard you try to keep it down. In the same way, no matter how hard you try to keep anger inside, or force it down, it will come back up.

So don't try to hide your anger. You'll only end up staying angry for a much longer time than you would have if you had acknowledged it. You need to express your angry feelings, although not with hostile actions or words. Talk it out with a friend, parent, or other trusted person. You'll find that your anger will go away a lot more quickly that way than if you keep it hidden.

enough on her plate trying to support the family that she didn't need to hear about Carol's problems.

In fact, when her mother had asked Carol if she minded the late-night work hours, Carol hadn't been able to explain how she felt. Although the new work hours really did bother Carol, she kept her feelings to herself. And her suppressed anger surfaced in the form of headaches and stomachaches.

The mind's effect on the body. When you suppress your emotions, you can make yourself physically ill. Holding in anger causes many different problems, including dizziness, teeth grinding, and tensed, aching muscles.

"Be not angry that you cannot make others as you wish them to be, since you cannot make yourself as you wish to be."

–Thomas A. Kempis

Suppressed anger can also make you sick with an ulcer, a stomachache, or a headache.

In Carol's case, she began to feel better after working for a while with a family therapist. He helped Carol talk about her troubles and learn skills to help her deal with her new situation.

Low self-esteem. Sometimes, kids who are feeling overwhelmed by stressful situations direct their anger inward. This typically occurs with people who have low self-esteem. They become angry with themselves, often putting themselves down and discouraging themselves with thoughts like "I'm really a loser" or ""I can't do anything right." Their low self-esteem makes it hard for them to deal with everyday stresses of life or to believe other people could possibly like them.

Self-esteem issues can arise anytime, and can really take a toll on a person's well-being.

Self-esteem issues can develop at any time. Some girls struggle with their feelings when the family goes through a divorce. Others become unhappy with the way their bodies change during puberty or obsess over their weight, believing they are too fat or too thin. Perfectionists who have high expectations for themselves become angry when they don't meet their goals. When low self-esteem issues combine with difficulty expressing anger and other emotional problems, serious eating disorders can result.

Anger

Eating disorders. One of the most serious disorders linked with anger and low self-esteem issues is anorexia nervosa. The disorder, in which a person has an obsessive desire to lose weight, affects mostly girls. In an effort to control something in life, a girl with anorexia nervosa severely restricts the amount of food she eats and constantly exercises to keep the pounds off. But no matter how much weight she loses, she believes she needs to lose more.

A similar eating disorder is bulimia, which involves the desire for extreme weight loss. However, the bulimic person overeats and then makes herself throw up the consumed food so she won't gain any weight.

Both of these eating disorders can result in life-threatening weight loss, because their victims don't get enough nutrients from food. But without proper medical treatment, the victims of these emotional disorders don't recognize that they are in danger of killing themselves.

Overeating has also been linked to teens with problems dealing with anger. A professor of behavioral science at the University of Texas Health Science Center, William Mueller, headed a study that found that teens who had trouble expressing anger were likely to have eating disorders and an unhealthy increase in weight. "They tend to isolate themselves,

Anorexia usually develops in girls who are ages twelve-through twenty-five-years-old. Most victims of this disorder are perfectionists who do not cope well with change, including the natural change that occurs when their bodies undergo puberty.[1]

watch TV or read rather than connecting with their friends," he noted in the study.[2]

Depression. Girls with low self-esteem and suppressed anger are also at risk for developing clinical depression. Its symptoms include feelings of sadness, hopelessness, and fatigue that last over a long period of time—weeks, months, or longer. People diagnosed with depression will withdraw from activities with friends, family, and others. They may stop doing school work or going to school. Depression interferes with a person's ability to socialize with other people. Major depressive disorder affects an estimated 5 percent of teens in the United States.[3]

Severe depression can distort thinking and lead to self-destructive behavior such as drug and alcohol abuse. Severely depressed individuals may hurt themselves by cutting or even try to kill themselves. If not treated, clinical depression can

Depression can become quite serious. If you think you or a friend may be depressed, ask for help from a trusted adult.

Some Symptoms of Depression

1. Loss of interest in favorite activities or hobbies
2. Ongoing feelings of sadness and hopelessness
3. Easily irritated and angered
4. Feelings of worthlessness or guilt
5. Low energy
6. Stomachaches and headaches
7. Difficulty relating to people socially
8. Changes in eating or sleeping habits
9. Trouble concentrating or following a conversation

lead to suicide, which is the third leading cause of death among fifteen- to twenty-five-year-olds.[4]

Get help. If you believe that you or a friend may be suffering from clinical depression, don't ignore your feelings. It is very important that you do something to get help for anyone who shows signs of depression. Talk to a trusted friend or your parents, school counselor, religious leader, or other adult. If you are not sure who can help, you can call the suicide prevention hotline shown on page 61.

When other people know what's going on in your or your friend's life, they will be able to help. Disorders such as anorexia nervosa, bulimia, and clinical depression are treatable. With medication and therapy, as well as support from family and friends, it is possible for victims of these disorders to overcome them.

Mean Girls and Bullies

> *When Kathy entered the seventh grade, she suddenly became a social outcast. She had no one to eat lunch with and was never invited to parties. The other girls teased her about her glasses, her body, and the way she dressed. "There was a lot of plotting and scheming behind people's backs. It was horrible," she later recalled. "I don't remember anything I learned that year."[1]*

Kathy's treatment by the other girls in her school is called "relational aggression." The term refers to a nonphysical form of bullying in which relationships are used to harm another person. When guys want to hurt other guys, they usually do so with their fists. But when girls want to hurt other girls, they are more likely to use words. They spread rumors and gossip, pass notes, talk about the outcast behind her back, and find other ways to be cruel.

Girls who are bullies use their power to abuse others. Their victims may not suffer from physical

Girls may pick on another girl because of what she wears or how she looks.

pain, but they do suffer emotionally from the bullying. According to the National Association of School Psychologists, each day more than 160,000 children refuse to go to school because they know that one or more bullies are waiting for them.[2] Being teased or physically threatened by peers saps the victim's self-esteem and make her feel helpless to stop the attacks.

Use anger to stand up for yourself. If a girl is being constantly teased by bullies, says psychologist Sharon Lamb, she can use her anger to stand up for herself. If she doesn't, then she will go on being victimized. The girl should respond to her tormentor by asserting herself, saying something like, "What you are doing is hurtful, and there is no good reason to treat me this way."[3] When confronting a bully, she should also try to hide her anger. Bullies feed off of the reactions they get from their victims. If the person doesn't react, they are likely to find someone else to target.

Cyberbullying Is a Serious Problem

A 2004 survey by i-Safe America of 1,500 fourth through eighth graders reported:

- 42 percent of them had been bullied online
- 35 percent had been threatened online
- 53 percent said hurtful things to others online
- 58 percent did not tell their parents or any other adult about being bullied[4]

It's tough feeling like the odd one out. Stay strong, and look for friends who accept you for who you are.

When Kathy was having trouble with bullies at school, she found her parents always willing to listen. She could talk about how she was hurting, and appreciated their concern.

According to Kathy, she learned a lot about her experience and now tries to treat everyone she knows with respect. She said, "I catch myself when I want to say something mean, and I stop because I know what it feels like to be on the other side."[5]

If you or someone you know is being bullied at school, you need to get help. Even

> "You can stand tall without standing on someone. You can be a victor without having victims."
>
> —Harriet Woods

Bullying on the Web

In recent years, "cyberbullies" have humiliated victims using instant messaging, e-mails, chat rooms, Web sites, and blogs to gossip and spread rumors. A twelve-year-old student from Massachusetts explains:

> "It gets pretty ugly in terms of how [girls] treat each other. They spread rumors that aren't necessarily true. It basically has to do with being jealous of how popular someone is. I think it's just as harmful as physical violence. The difference is this is a little less likely to be seen by teachers. You can just break up a fight. This is a lot more complicated."[6]

though you may find it hard to do, talk to an adult—your parents, a teacher, or the principal. Schools take bullying seriously and have a plan in place for dealing with it. Although it can be difficult to get involved, if you witness someone else being bullied, don't stand by silently. Stand up for the victim if you can. However, if you feel as though you will place yourself in a dangerous position by doing so, report the incident to a teacher as soon as possible.

If you don't do anything about what's making you angry, your anger will build up inside. Find a positive way to deal with the situation.

Don't Flip Out!

As Lydia was walking down the hall, two girls—Alisha and Bianca—bumped into her. Alisha gave a short laugh and continued walking, but Bianca stopped. She glared at Lydia in mock indignation, and asked, "Why are you such a klutz?" Everyone else in the hall stopped and stared.

Lydia felt her face burning. Alisha and Bianca had been giving her a hard time at school for the past six weeks and she was sick and tired of it. Her first urge was to give Bianca a hard shove that would send her sprawling. At that moment Lydia recognized it was time to apply some anger management techniques.

You can manage your angry feelings if you take charge right at the start. The anger management techniques that follow can help you keep a handle on your anger:

Recognize. The first rule for getting along with others is being able to recognize what makes you angry. Anger often occurs when you feel frustrated over something you can't control and that is important to you. The moment you feel that first flush of anger, you can make

Put a stop to your urge to lash out in anger. Recognize when you are ready to flip out—and make yourself relax.

yourself stop, step back, and use self-calming techniques—before you blow your top.

Relax. To keep yourself from acting out on your anger, take several deep breaths. Then, silently and slowly, count to ten, taking a deep breath with each number. Focus on making yourself relax. The time it takes for you to slowly count to ten will give you some time to cool off and relax. This way, you can stop the fight-or-flight reaction

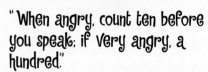

"When angry, count ten before you speak; if very angry, a hundred."

–Thomas Jefferson

Managing Your Anger

There are better ways to manage your anger than being physically aggressive, says the American Psychological Association. It is really not a good idea to punch or hit your pillow when you're mad because you'll develop the habit of wanting to strike out with aggression whenever you're frustrated and angry. Some alternative behaviors include:

Distract yourself: Think of a soothing place you'd rather be. Go there for just a few moments or meditate.

Express your anger: Talk to the person you have an issue with, but only after you've calmed down. That way, you'll be able to explain your case in an assertive way.

Forgive and try to forget. If you can't talk it out, ask yourself if what's annoying you will matter to you a week from now. If not, then simply drop the issue.[1]

and any impulse to be aggressive. Focusing on counting can also distract you from the person or event making you angry in the first place.

Problem solve. As you focus on your breathing, think about your options. Consider the consequences of being aggressive or violent. For example, if Lydia were to hit Bianca, what would be the outcome? There would probably be more hostility between the two girls. A physical fight could result in detention or suspension from school.

Change the environment. Give yourself time to sort things out. If you need to, remove yourself from a tense situation.

While away, use one of the following techniques to help you calm yourself. Exercising and physical activities such as kicking a soccer ball, dancing, or jumping rope might make you feel better. Or sing along with your favorite music. You might also call a friend and talk things over with her. Sometimes talking about your feelings can make them less powerful. And having another person who can empathize with what you are going through can help, too.

RETHINK Your Anger

The Institute for Mental Health Initiatives, based in Washington, D.C., recommends an anger management technique called RETHINK. It stands for Recognize, Empathize, Think, Hear, Integrate, Notice and Keep.

R The moment you recognize you are angry, you can begin taking steps to regain control of yourself.

E When you empathize with the other person, you put yourself in their shoes and try to see the situation as they see it.

T With that new information you can think about the options you have for dealing with the situation.

H When you take the time to hear what the other person is saying, that gives you additional clues about why the person is acting the way he or she is.

I Then, you can integrate this information—that is, combine it with everything else you already know—in deciding what to do next.

N Notice means to pay attention to what it feels like to be angry.

K Keep refers to keeping your attention on the problem.[2]

In Lydia's case, she spun on her heel and headed off to her next class. However, she resolved that she would talk to Alisha and Bianca separately later that day. After Lydia cooled down,

she arranged to meet with Bianca in the school library. Bianca seemed calmer, too. In a quiet, but assertive voice, Lydia explained that she preferred being friends with Bianca, but wouldn't accept being treated rudely. Although Lydia had no guarantee that her words would change Bianca's behavior, she felt better about herself for asserting herself.

Communicate. The problem won't go away if you ignore it. The best way to get someone to really listen to you is

Put Your Anger in Writing

You might try composing a letter to the person you're angry with. It should contain everything that made you mad—don't hold anything back. You aren't actually going to mail this letter, but it should include everything you feel like saying. The next day, read it over. When you have finished, write another letter on the same topic, putting in any new thoughts you have. Then, on the following day, read your first two letters one more time before writing a third, last letter. When you finish, tear up all three letters and throw them away— along with your anger—into the trash.

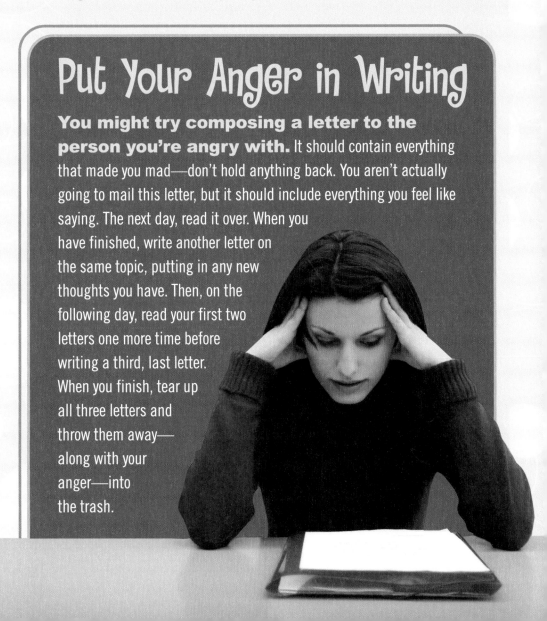

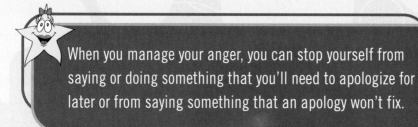

When you manage your anger, you can stop yourself from saying or doing something that you'll need to apologize for later or from saying something that an apology won't fix.

to not make that person defensive. Name-calling, trading insults, trying to tell the other person what you think she is feeling, and refusing to speak to someone will only make a bad situation worse.

Choosing Your Battles

Thirteen-year-old Sara decided she was spending too much time arguing and fighting with others. So she came up with an idea of how to stop. She would rate the importance of a potential argument or disagreement on a scale of 1 to 10 (with 1 being the lowest and 10 the highest priority). For example, when she was about to have an argument with her sister over whose turn it was to do the dishes, she might rank that at #1. A discussion with her parents about curfew could be #5, while being accused of cheating by her teacher would rank as a #10. Using this system, she decided to argue only when conflicts rated at #5 or above.

Sara had learned that by deciding to "choose her battles"—letting less important issues go—she had fewer conflicts with other people. She also found that in the situations where she did stand her ground, people took her more seriously.[3]

Resolving Conflicts

What can you do if someone else is angry at you? Experts say that when someone else is yelling, you should stay calm yourself. Avoid the temptation of yelling back. Choose your words carefully, and respond in a low and even tone. Once you succeed in getting the other person to calm down, you can begin working on at least a temporary solution to the problem. However, if your attempts to get the person to calm down fail, you should leave the situation. This is especially true if you are being verbally abused or fear that the person will harm you. Before attempting to have a conversation, it is best to allow the other person to calm down.

Steps to resolve conflicts. When trying to resolve a conflict—whether with your parents, your friends, or your siblings—take some time to cool off first. Then use the following steps:

- **Define the problem.** What, exactly, is the conflict about? Determine whether the fight is one single incident or a sign of a larger problem that one of you is having.

- **Talk about the problem.** Don't try to place blame on the other person. Just try to find out how the other person

is feeling. Use I-messages to tell him or her what is bothering you. Listen carefully to what the other person has to say. Take responsibility for your hurtful words and actions, and apologize if you were wrong.

- **Think about solutions.** What are some things you can do to solve the problem? What can the other person do? Brainstorm a list of solutions that would resolve your conflict.

- **Evaluate the alternatives.** Come to an agreement on a solution that both of you can agree with. You may need to negotiate with each other to find a solution to your conflict that is acceptable to both of you. The word negotiate means to try to reach an agreement through discussion and compromise. When you compromise, you are giving up something important to you in exchange for reaching an agreement. For negotiation to work, you have to approach things with an open mind, and be willing to listen to the other person. You can't negotiate effectively if either of you are upset or angry.

- **Follow through.** Choose a solution and carry it out. Once you've agreed on the best way to handle things, stick with your decision.

Peer Mediation. Many schools have instituted programs in which two people having a conflict come to an agreement with the help of a third person. This other person acts as a mediator in their dispute. A mediator is a person who listens to both person's complaints and then tries to help them resolve their disagreement.

Quiz: Making Choices

If handled properly, nearly every issue that could make you angry has outcomes that would improve the situation. How you choose to resolve them determines whether you've made things better. How would you handle the following situations?

1. Your girlfriend tells you she is mad at you for not returning her call. You realize your sister never gave you the message. Would you

   A. Not say a word about this to your sister.
   B. Ask your sister if your friend had called while you were out.
   C. Get even with your sister by not telling her the next time she misses a phone call.

2. Your teacher gives you a "C" on a paper that you think deserved a "B." Do you

   A. Go home and cry.
   B. Ask the teacher to explain why you got the grade you did.
   C. Rip the paper up and tell your friends how bad the teacher is.

3. Your classmate asks to copy your homework. Do you

   A. Let her, even though you don't like the idea.
   B. Tell her you'd rather not, but you'd be glad to help with hers.
   C. Tell her you're not a cheater like she is.

4. Your friend wants to go to the movies but you both want to see something different. Do you

   A. Go to the movie she suggested.
   B. Tell her that you really want to see something else and try to work it out.
   C. See the movie she suggested, but complain later about how stupid it was.

In each case, the B answer would have put you on the right track.

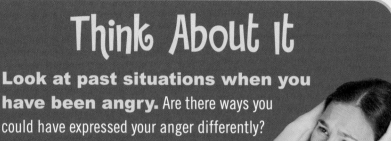
Peer mediation programs involve training a few students within the school in conflict resolution techniques. To help resolve conflicts, these peer mediators listen and ask open-ended questions. They don't give advice or take sides. And they don't have the power to determine punishments. Mediators do not come up with the solutions. Their job is to help the two students who have a conflict come to their own solutions for resolving their issues.

To get good results in resolving conflicts, be assertive. That means you work on being direct, but also friendly. Make it clear that you want to be treated fairly and you will do the same.

Using Your Anger

Yesterday, Janelle learned that money students had raised in the talent show wouldn't be given to the hurricane relief agency chosen by the student council. Mrs. Pollister, the teacher advising the council, had overruled the idea because she had never heard of the organization. Janelle was furious that Mrs. Pollister would overrule the students' decision about where they wanted their donation to go.

When you feel something is not right, anger can spur you to take action. You may feel angry because you think your decisions, beliefs, or values have been ignored or insulted. Or you may decide that a situation is wrong and you want to change it. However, if you want to be successful about bringing about change, your attitude is important.

In Janelle's case, she let some time pass in order to allow herself to calm down. Then she talked to a few other student council members and asked for their help. Together, the group sought out Mrs. Pollister and politely asked to have a talk

Take that anger and USE IT!

with her. In a calm voice, Janelle explained that she knew a lot about the relief agency since her aunt worked for the organization. She gave the teacher copies of information she had found on the charity group's Web site. Then the group submitted a petition to Mrs. Pollister asking her to reconsider her decision. Janelle felt good that she stood up for herself and the other student council members.

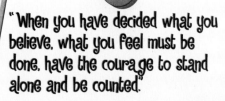

"When you have decided what you believe, what you feel must be done, have the courage to stand alone and be counted."

—Eleanor Roosevelt

When you feel angry because you believe someone is not treating you fairly, you need to speak up and make your voice heard. But you also want to present your case in a way that will produce positive results.

Anger Can Be Helpful When It...

1. Motivates you to accomplish a goal

2. Pushes yourself to solve a problem

3. Makes you see that you or someone else has not been treated fairly

4. Gives you courage and self-confidence to assert yourself or stand up for your rights

5. Pushes you to band together with other people to demand change or social justice

Anger can be a motivator to get a group to act.

Dealing with your angry feelings can be complicated. You want to manage and express your anger so your point of view is clearly understood. And you want the other side to be willing to listen. The best way to do that in a conflict with another individual is to be respectful. Explain your points calmly and clearly. Be assertive—not aggressive—when you stand up for what you believe to be right. Make it clear that you think you've been treated unfairly and will not accept unfair treatment.

The same holds true when you're bothered by an issue that affects many people. Do something! Make a plan, share your concerns with others, and get people to work with you to bring about change. When a group of people gets angry over a

It is not wrong to get angry. But it is wrong to express your anger in ways that hurt others or damage property.

Anger

The Woman's Right to Vote

It was the early part of the twentieth century, and one group of women in the United States was very angry. The women wanted to be able to vote in federal elections, and they couldn't. Since the 1800s, women had organized and petitioned for suffrage—the right to vote in political elections. As early as 1878, an amendment granting woman suffrage had been introduced in Congress. But it never passed, despite being reintroduced again and again.

On January 10, 1917, members of the National Woman's Party decided to take their anger over the situation to President Woodrow Wilson. On that day, suffragettes began to picket the White House, an action that women had never taken before. Protests and nonstop picketing—except on Sundays—would continue through June 1919, when Congress finally passed the amendment. Many NWP members would be arrested and jailed for their protest activities. But they continued to stand up for what they believed in.

These efforts contributed to the president calling on Congress in 1918 to pass a suffrage amendment. The 19th Amendment, which gave women the right to vote in state and federal elections, was officially ratified on August 18, 1920.

situation, they can make a difference. Many social injustices have been addressed by people expressing their anger through peaceful marches and protests.

Good anger management skills can help you in your relationships with others both now and in the future. When you know how to express your angry feelings in a constructive way, you will feel better about yourself. And others will also respect you, too.

Chapter 1. I'm So Mad . . .

1. Rachel Simmons, *Odd Girl Speaks Out: Girls Write About Bullies, Cliques, Popularity, and Jealousy* (New York: Harcourt, 2004), p. 143.

2. "Anger and Violence in Public Schools Documented in New SPH Survey," *Harvard University Gazette*, October 22, 1998, <www.hno.harvard.edu/gazette/1998/10.22/AngerandViolenc.html> (December 19, 2007).

Chapter 2. How Do You Show Anger?

1. Adapted from David J. Decker and Mike Obsatz, "Your Anger Index: How Angry and Hostile Are You?" *ANGEResources*, July 12, 2006, <www.angeresources.com/angerindex.html> (July 13, 2007).

2. Clayton E. Tucker-Ladd, "Chapter 7: Anger and Aggression," *Psychological Self-Help*, 2006, <www.psychologicalselfhelp.org> (July 13, 2007).

3. "Violence Is a Learned Behavior, Say Researchers at Wake Forest University," *ScienceDaily*, November 9, 2000, <http://www.sciencedaily.com/releases/2000/11/001106061128.htm> (July 13, 2007).

Chapter 3. When Friends Make You Mad

1. Quoted in Nanci Hellmich, "Caught in the Catty Corner," *USA Today*, April 9, 2002, p. D-1.

Chapter 5. Keeping Your Cool with Adults

1. Quoted in Michael G. Conner, "Why Do Teenagers Get So Angry?" *Family News*, 2003, <www.crisiscounseling.com/Articles/AngryChilden.htm> (July 16, 2007).

Chapter 6. When You Keep Anger Inside

1. "Eating Disorders," *University Health Services, Princeton University*, n.d., <http://www.princeton.edu/uhs/ih_Q_A_eating_disorders.html#anorexia> (July 16, 2007).

2. Quoted in Lee Bowman, "Study: Mismanaged Anger Makes for Fat Teens," *Scripps Howard News Service*, March 5, 2004, <www.shns.com/shns/ g_index2.cfm?action-detail&pk=TEENAGER-03-05-04> (July 13, 2007).

3. "Antidepressant Medications for Children and Adolescents: Information for Parents and Caregivers," *National Institute of*

Health, December 18, 2007, <http://www.nimh.nih.gov/
health/topics/child-and-adolescent-mental-health/
antidepressant-medications-for-children-and-adolescents-
information-for-parents-and-caregivers.shtml> (December 19,
2007).

4. "Suicide: Facts at a Glance," *U.S. Centers for Disease Control
    and Prevention*, Summer 2007, <http://www.cdc.gov/ncipc/
    dvp/suicide/SuicideDataSheet.pdf> (December 19, 2007).

Chapter 7. Mean Girls and Bullies

1. Quoted in Nanci Hellmich, "Caught in the Catty Corner,"
    USA Today, April 9, 2002, p. D–1.

2. U.S. Department of Education, "Exploring the Nature and
    Prevention of Bullying," *Ed.gov*, November 13, 2007,
    <http://www.ed.gov/admins/lead/safety/training/bullying/bul-
    lying_pg14.html> (December 19, 2007).

3. Quoted in Nanci Hellmich, "Caught in the Catty Corner,"
    USA Today, April 9, 2002, p. D–1.

4. Adapted from "Cyber Bullying: Statistics and Tips," *i-SAFE*,
    n.d., <http://www.isafe.org/channels/sub.php?ch=
    op&sub_id=media_cyber_bullying> (December 19, 2007).

5. Quoted in Nanci Hellmich, "Caught in the Catty Corner,"
    USA Today, April 9, 2002, p. D–1.

6. Quoted in Gail Spector, "Author to Speak on Ways to Deal
    with Girl Bullies," *Boston Globe*, December 15, 2002, p. 3.

Chapter 8. Don't Flip Out!

1. Adapted from Alissa MacMillan. "Reduce Your Rage," *Redbook*,
    August 1999, p. 140.

2. Leanne Spengler. "Containing Anger—Rethink," *University of
    Missouri Outreach and Extension*, Winter 1997–98,
    <http://extension.missouri.edu/missing-piece/articles/
    rethink.html> (January 10, 2008).

3. Richard Carlson, *Don't Sweat the Small Stuff: For Teens* (New
    York: Hyperion, 2000), p. 37.

adrenaline—A hormone secreted from the adrenal glands when the body is under stress.

amygdala—The small, almond-shaped part of the brain that controls memory and emotions.

anger—A strong emotion characterized by annoyance or displeasure.

assertive—Able to express one's own needs and wishes while respecting those of others.

compromise—An agreement in which both sides agree to give up something in order to resolve a conflict.

conflict—A struggle that results from disagreements about needs, wishes, demands, or opinions.

depression—A feeling of intense sadness and hopelessness.

eating disorder—An abnormal or disturbed eating habit such as anorexia nervosa or bulimia.

fight-or-flight instinct—The initial reaction of the body when a person feels threatened.

hormone—A substance produced by the cells of the body that influences behavior and mood.

mediator—A person trained in techniques to help people in conflict reach peaceful agreements.

negotiate—To come to an agreement through discussion and compromise.

personality—The behavior and emotional characteristics of a person.

puberty—The developmental stage in which a person's body goes through the physical changes in becoming an adult.

self-esteem—Respect for or satisfaction you have about yourself.

stress—Physical and emotional strain caused by external forces or circumstances.

therapist—A person who works with individuals to solve relationship difficulties; therapists can be psychologists, psychiatrists, or others with specialized degrees in family relationships.

FURTHER READING

Karnes, Erika V. *Mean Chicks, Cliques, and Dirty Tricks: A Real Girls Guide to Getting Through the Day with Smarts and Style.* Avon, Mass.: Adams Media, 2004.

Verdick, Elizabeth, and Marjorie Lisovskis. *How to Take the Grrrr Out of Anger*, Minneapolis, Minn.: Free Spirit Publishing, 2000.

Wilde, Jerry. *More Hot Stuff to Help Kids Chill Out: The Anger and Stress Management Book.* Richmond, Ind.: LGR Publishing, 2000.

INTERNET ADDRESSES

The American Psychological Association
http://www.apa.org/topics/controlanger.html

It's My Life
http://pbskids.org/itsmylife/emotions/anger/index.html

Nemours Foundation for Children's Health Media
http://www.kidshealth.org/question/emotions/deal_with_anger.html

HOTLINE TELEPHONE NUMBERS

National Domestic Violence Hotline
1-800-799-SAFE (1-800-799-7233)

National Suicide Prevention Lifeline
1-800-273-TALK (1-800-273-8255)

CONTRiBUTORS

Author **Gail Snyder** is a freelance writer who has written ten books for young adults. She lives in Pennsylvania with her husband, Hal Marcovitz, who is coauthor of this book, and their daughters. Gail is also the author of two other titles in the Flip-It-Over Guides to Teen Emotions series.

Series advisor **Dr. Carroll Izard** is the Trustees Distinguished Professor of Psychology at the University of Delaware. His research and writing focuses on the development of emotion knowledge and emotion regulation and their contributions to social and emotional competence. He is author or editor of seventeen books (one of which won a national award) and more than one hundred articles in scientific journals. Dr. Izard is a fellow of both national psychological associations and the American Association for the Advancement of Science. He is the winner of the American Psychological Association's G. Stanley Hall Award and an international exchange fellowship from the National Academy of Sciences.

A Guys' Guide to Anger; A Girls' Guide to Anger
ISBN-13: 978-0-7660-2853-1   ISBN-10: 0-7660-2853-4

A Guys' Guide to Conflict; A Girls' Guide to Conflict
ISBN-13: 978-0-7660-2852-4   ISBN-10: 0-7660-2852-6

A Guys' Guide to Jealousy; A Girls' Guide to Jealousy
ISBN-13: 978-0-7660-2854-8   ISBN-10: 0-7660-2854-2

A Guys' Guide to Loneliness; A Girls' Guide to Loneliness
ISBN-13: 978-0-7660-2856-2   ISBN-10: 0-7660-2856-9

A Guys' Guide to Love; A Girls' Guide to Love
ISBN-13: 978-0-7660-2855-5   ISBN-10: 0-7660-2855-0

A Guys' Guide to Stress; A Girls' Guide to Stress
ISBN-13: 978-0-7660-2857-9   ISBN-10: 0-7660-2857-7

GUYS!

KEEP OUT

Nothing But Girl Talk Ahead– You've Been Warned!